NO ONE EVER GAVE A B

Infamous gunslinger, Porter .... the Ute War Chief, Redbone, to help him no matter what. Now that the Chief's daughter has been kidnapped by the desperado Matamoros, and that favor is getting called in at a most inopportune time. Of course, Porter's closest friends—buffalo soldier Quincy Cuthbert Jackson and card sharp Roxy LeJuene—are coming along too. Too late, they learn that chasing down the kidnapper is only the beginning of a deadly path.

As they follow the Old Spanish Trail, secrets threaten to tear the rescuer's bond apart and an unexpected stowaway increases the danger. Clues to a more sinister plot quickly unfold, and dark native magics breath terrible spells over their mission. Can Porter and his friends resolve their differences and save the girl or will they sacrifice more than life somewhere along the dark trail?

— CRAZY HORSES

To Blake

Shoot Straight

CRAZY HORSES

David J. West

***

David J. West

LOSTREALMS PRESS

Sign up for Burnt Offerings and get a free ebook!

FOR KEVIN MOLETT

CHAPTERS

The wildest colts make the best horses. — Plutarch

1. Dark Repercussions

Porter and Quincy shared a whiskey in the Oasis saloon. It was as fine a place as they could hang their hats this side of Salt Lake or, for that matter, Porter's own spread at the Point of the Mountain. Porter had his feet up on the table. He hadn't enjoyed Valley-Tan whiskey this good in what . . . two weeks?

He was on his third shot when Port realized he hadn't been home in nearly a month, my how time flies when you're chasing outlaws, dodging bullets and just staying alive in the middle of a hellish desert.

Quincy and Roxy sprawled at the table directly beside him.

Roxy idly stirred her tea, shooing away a handful of flies curiously intent on sampling her honey-sweetened drink. "I wish I would have thought to get my faro deck from that canyon," she said. "I could be making a fortune instead of rotting here with you two."

"Money isn't a problem, is it?" Quincy asked with a laugh. He jingled his own purse.

She smirked and shook her head. "No, I just didn't want to lose the deck. We were in such a rush to get out of there, I plum forgot it." She looked wistfully at the smudged window.

"I've got to get on back to Salt Lake and see if there is any news for me. I don't suppose you two want to come along?" Porter looked hopeful. Truth was he enjoyed company, just most folks didn't enjoy his. Being known far and wide as 'The Destroying Angel' made the social graces a little more difficult.

Quincy arched his brow at Roxy, but she shook her head. "I can't go back. At least not yet."

Porter nodded, asking, "What do you want me to say when I see him? You know if he asks me—which I believe he will."

"Just tell him that I love him and Mama, but I don't know that the life there is what I want."

Porter frowned. It wasn't a conversation he wanted to have.

"I need to see the world. Maybe I'll go to San Francisco. I think I'd like to run my own place. Something like this," she said gesturing about the saloon.

"You could run your own here. You've got enough cash you could rent and open a place," suggested Porter.

"Now we're talking," said Quincy.

She shook her head. "Not here. You know I couldn't stay here; it would be bad for Papa if I did. I need to be far, far away."

"You know I'd go with you anywhere," said Quincy. His hands reached across the table to hold hers.

She leaned back out of reach, looked at him with a half-smile and sad eyes. "Maybe I need to be alone for a little while."

Quincy frowned. "All right," he said softly, sliding his hands off the table and deep into his pockets.

Porter was about to say something, but went suddenly quiet. Instinct whispered there was trouble nearby, old habits die hard and Port's hand went to his .45's pommel. He watched the batwing doors like a hawk about to pounce.

A tall man came through, two burly men flanking him. The posse members each held rifles ready, but not yet pointed at anyone. The tall man had a long, pronounced handlebar mustache, dark, deep-set eyes with an imperious cast to them, and a tarnished tin star on his chest. "Porter," he said, motioning for his quarry to stand, "I got you now. The gallows won't be cheated any longer. I'm finally going to arrest you for murder and conspiracy." A wicked smile peaked out from beneath that long drooping mustache. It was plain he was thrilled to be in the moment. Like a dog that finally found a bone.

Quincy and Roxy were tense, ready to draw weapons and throw down with the accuser and his posse, but Porter was relaxed. He didn't bother to even take his feet off the table he had them stretched out on. "Conspiracy? Murder?" chuckled Porter. "Whose? You got a weapon? A motive? Hell, have you even got a body this time, Shaw?"

The incredibly brief drop of Shaw's face before his stoic mask returned showed he had neither body nor any other evidence. He must have been gambling he could railroad Porter into the local poke and then produce evidence or a confession. He should have known better.

Porter laughed. "Roxy, Quint, this here is Brody Shaw. One time territorial marshal—"

"I'm still the territorial marshal!" Shaw shouted.

"—Full time jackass," continued Porter softly.

"Keep laughing Danite! But, I know you're involved in the deaths of Captain Thorn, Reverend Mort, and countless others. Let's go. Right now. Peaceful like." He motioned toward the door.

Porter didn't budge, but blew smoke from his cheroot in Shaw's direction. "Sure, you are. How many times do you think the governor is going to accept your wild accusations and clear lack of results?"

Shaw's left eye twitched. "I've eventually captured and hung every man I've ever had a mind to go after. I'll get you, too, one of these days."

"If I had a dime for every time someone told me that, I'd be a rich man."

Quincy interjected, "You are a rich man."

"See?" chuckled Porter.

Shaw's posse looked like they were getting antsy and fidgeted with their rifles. Quincy and Roxy had their own guns ready. Shaw held a hand up saying, "Your time is gonna come."

"So, you don't have any evidence, do you?"

Shaw smirked. "Maybe I don't have anything yet, but I do have the governor's approval to bring in your mangy hide soon as I do have a body. With what folks are calling the Thorn massacre, I'm bound to find a body soon enough. You really think I won't find one of those sixty-three missing men?"

Porter looked at him suddenly, eyes narrowing like he was a rattler about to strike.

"That's right. Maybe you didn't count. But between Captain Lucas Thorn's command, Reverend Mort and his accompanying congregation, and even those outlaws—the Cotterells. All them are dead so far as rumor goes. No one has seen any of them in a week. I suspect you're behind it, since you and your friends are the only ones who have been seen since."

Porter grinned. "You really think I killed sixty-three people this last week? Just me?"

"Oh, I am sure you had some help," Shaw growled, looking at Quincy and Roxy. "Maybe more. I still aim to prove you were at Mountain Meadows too. I'm sure it's the same kind of bloody-handed work you're known for."

Porter grunted. "I never killed anyone that didn't need killing."

"Someday evidence will come out that you were there."

Porter abruptly stood up.

Shaw's two deputies ducked out the doors in a panic, but Shaw stood facing the gunslinger, ready to draw if the Porter did first. Which he didn't.

"I've got plenty of witnesses say I was in Salt Lake during that and those bodies were left out to rot for anyone to find. Now, you go and find these missing sixty-three bodies before you accuse me again. 'Til then, stay outta my way."

Shaw backed up toward the batwing doors, with his hands held high. "Oh, I'm a backing up all right. But, this time you've left far too big a mess to get out of. I'll find them bodies and then you're gonna hang. I'm a watching you."

Porter scoffed. "You best find yourself a new hobby."

"I ain't forgetting. I'll find that evidence. I know you've done it. I am going to do the world a service when I bring you to justice."

"It'll be a tough go for short dough, Peckerwood."

"I'm gonna see you hang, Danite."

"Go hang yourself," Porter muttered.

Shaw snorted and disappeared through the doors.

Quincy shook his head saying, "Damn, I thought you were about to cut the wolf loose there."

"I suppose I was."

Roxy looked to Porter. "Sixty-three people?" she whispered.

Porter shook his head and said, "There ain't no witnesses. Redbone won't ever talk and there ain't gonna be anything or anyone to ever find and that's that. They're all under tons of rock, or dragged away and hidden by the Utes. I got me a clean conscience on dead murderers."

"You sure?" she asked in a whisper.

"I throw my regrets out with the trash most every night. Doesn't do a body a lick of good to hang on to regrets. I got precious few that linger and I'll be damned if I'll keep one for the likes of those pukes—Thorn and Mort."

"I back you up one hundred percent, Port," said Quincy. "But, suppose he does find evidence somewhere? Like what if anyone besides us and Redbone survived that canyon gunfight?"

"Redbone would have mopped them all up. We got nothing to worry about. We just keep our word together and this will all blow over like everything else."

"What else have you done, that just blew over?" asked Roxy, pointedly.

Porter leaned in closer, like he was about to reveal a great secret, then smirked, saying, "Lots of things."

A man burst through the saloon doors, setting them swinging. His eyes were wide as pie plates and a slick sheen of sweat covered his panicky brow. "Marshal Rockwell! Marshal Rockwell! There's a bloody Indian riding into town and he is a sight to see! You need to do something!"

Porter took one more sip of his whiskey and stood up. "Notice how he didn't call for Shaw?" He laughed.

"Porter!" snapped Roxy. "This could be serious."

"It ain't!" He snapped. "Just a bunch of fool townies panicking."

"Well, I'm going to go look."

Porter took another sip of whiskey, licked his lips in satisfaction then stretched like a jungle cat before he strode out the batwing doors.

Townsfolk were scurrying for cover off the streets. Porter squinted against the setting sun at the dark rider approaching.

Whomever it was, he sure had the town in an uproar.

Quincy was at Port's side in a moment, as was Roxy. But it ended up being no worry for the three of them, at least not just yet.

There on the far end of the street, big as life was Redbone! He rode on a wounded pony, but the war-chief looked even worse. Bloody gashes covered his lean body. There were bullet wounds in his thigh and his shoulder oozed blood from beneath a stained rag of a bandage.

"What's going on, Chief? Did we miss someone up that canyon?" Porter asked, then realized what he said out loud and looked around just to be sure that Shaw wasn't nearby. Fortunately, he wasn't anywhere to be seen.

Redbone dismounted and almost fell to his knees. He had been weeping. Unthinkable that this man could cry, but there were tears stains running down his dirty, bloody face. "My daughter. They took my daughter."

Porter helped him stand and ushered him inside the saloon.

Several of the folk who had crowded inside at Redbone's approach now rushed out, and the proprietor tensed his jaw before mustering the courage to say something. "Mister Rockwell, sir. We don't serve their kind in here. It's bad enough you're having me serve the nigger, but the red-skin has got to wait outside like every other savage."

"Nigger?" questioned Quincy, pausing mid-swallow.

8

Porter's eyes flashed. "Savage? Hell, if you're worried about a savage you shouldn't a served me."

The barkeep paled, and then made himself busy elsewhere, disappearing into the backroom.

They helped Redbone to a seat at their table, and Roxy began cleaning his wounds with a rag, dipping it in the whiskey to sterilize it.

The big Ute didn't even start at the cold, burning touch of the alcohol.

"Who took your daughter?" asked Quincy.

"Matamoros. He had some Apache raiders with him and they rode into our village. Shot and killed many braves and took my daughter and others."

Roxy gasped and looked at Porter. "We need to do something."

Porter shrugged. "What? Matamoros must be halfway to Santa Fe by now. How long ago did this happen?"

Redbone grasped Porter by the shoulder. "Three days. But above on the highlands. I followed him this close, then came to get you. He should only be a day or two ahead of us."

"Is he heading for the Old Spanish Trail?"

Redbone nodded.

"He has too great a head start. I don't know that we can catch him, especially since you're wounded and all."

"Porter!" cried Roxy. "You have to help him."

"You are my Blood Brother, are you not? I need your help to get her back. I cannot let her go into slavery with those men. I will ride on no matter what my body is like. I will not slow down the pursuit."

Roxy gave Porter an encouraging nod of her head.

9

Porter rubbed at his beard and twisted his lips into a scowl. Redbone had him dead to rights. He had made the Blood Brother pact with the Ute chief and was honor bound to help. "Yeah. Wheat! Quint, I don't expect you to come along, but I'd sure appreciate having you."

Quincy nodded. "I ain't gonna miss this, no sir."

"What about me?" asked Roxy.

"Well, I figured you had sights to see, and your own life to live."

"This is gonna be an awful rough trip catching those desperadoes. It will be ugly. I don't know that you're up to this kind of chase."

"Shouldn't I be the judge of that?"

Porter shrugged again. "I didn't want to assume."

"But you assumed I wasn't capable?"

Redbone had a look of something other than pain on his face. "If the Lucky Woman wants to come, then she should come."

"Fine," growled Porter. "We better get our supplies together and quick, we need to tear down the miles between us as fast as we can."

Quincy nodded. "I'll go get our horses saddled and ready, if Roxy can get us some rations."

She nodded her head and hurried out the door.

Porter smirked and said, "All right, I'll get us the other supplies." He reached over the bar and grabbed an armful of Valley-Tan whiskey bottles. They clinked together, loudly.

Roxy stepped back into the saloon and glared at Porter in disapproval.

"We need these for medicinal purposes," he said, sheepishly.

Her eyebrows raised in silent judgment.

"Knock it off, I can drink if I want too, woman!"

"How is that going to help out in our circumstance?" she asked.

"You never know. And I never know when I'll be able to get another square drink!"

"Anything else?"

"Yeah, quit judging me and go get us those rations while I get some more ammunition and powder."

✲✲✲

Redbone was pleased that his Blood Brother and company were assembling so quickly. For white people, they moved with swift determination. Humbling as it was, he knew he had not made a rash decision in enlisting their aid, no matter how much he felt scorned by the rest of the whites.

2. Burning Bridges

In less than an hour, they were on the trail out of Price. Redbone guided them across the winding roads, over washed out streambeds and shortcuts through sage brush covered hills. They kept in a south easterly direction with the towering Book Cliffs on their left. They knew where to cross the many ravines that cut through the land, remnants of the spring flash floods. These trenches dug into the ground a dozen feet deep and nearly was wide in many places.

It was a familiar enough path, the same route they had so recently returned on coming back from the Lost Hoard venture. Luckily for them, they had had a full day to recuperate and rest, unlike Redbone. But the dogged war-chief would not complain nor give up. He stoically rocked to and fro on his horse, ignoring his pain and keeping them all on a good pace.

They camped the first night at a small boom town called Woodside. When they were almost asleep, they noticed riders coming into town and bedding down, not too far away on the far side of the town's one saloon. It wasn't too hard to guess who it was.

"Shaw," grumbled Porter, resting his chin upon his saddle. "That tenacious polecat. What's he expect to find following us?"

"Maybe he expects to find bodies," suggested Quincy.

Porter glared at Quincy with a growl.

Quincy played devil's advocate a moment. "Well, he ain't got anything else to go on. Sides, maybe he'd be some help if we catch up to Matamoros soon. Another few guns would be handy."

"That puke wouldn't help us in a gunfight against Lucifer himself, which is close enough to what Matamoros is. But better that he doesn't get any ideas or interrogate Matamoros either. We don't want him catching that bastard and questioning him before I use him up."

"Use him up?" asked Roxy.

"Kill," answered Porter bluntly.

She didn't respond.

They ran a cold camp, despite knowing full well Shaw knew they were there too.

A couple hours before dawn, Porter had them up and moving on down the trail in the cool semi-dark. It didn't slow Shaw down much though, by mid-morning they saw him in the distance following along with six or seven members in his posse.

"You think he'll do anything antagonistic out in this high lonesome?" asked Quincy.

Porter shook his head. "I doubt it, but he wants to ride our tails like ticks on a hound. He wants the answer to that mystery, and he won't get it by shooting us."

"What if wants to provoke a gun fight?" asked Roxy.

Porter had to think about that for a second. "Maybe, but he knows as well as anybody my reputation, so I doubt it." Porter laughed to himself. "Come to think of it, I do believe he has taken some potshots at me in the vain hope of proving my blessing wrong. Course they all missed and he can't admit to failing."

"You got a funny way of thinking Port," said Quincy.

13

Porter looked at him and shrugged.

"I mean, you laugh at death more than anyone I know. I suppose because you have that blessing. Makes you feel invulnerable, but I jest want to remind you the rest of us aren't invulnerable, so don't go getting us in any scrapes we can't get out of."

"Have I ever?"

Roxy silenced him. "Don't even."

"Fine, I'll make sure and slow down Shaw before he gets any closer."

They went on for another half mile until they came upon another deep ravine cut out by spring runoff. This one was too wide for horses except at a particularly narrow and deep bend. Here it had a stable little bridge made from pines out of the nearby mountains, lashed together with thongs of rawhide and a few spikes. It wasn't the best bridge ever made, but it sure wasn't the worst Port had ever ridden across.

Once they were all on the other side, Porter began worrying at the ground where the thing was lashed to a juniper stump. When he had all the anchors free, he motioned for the others to help him.

Porter and Quincy did the lion's share of the work, but the four of them helped heave the whole thing into the ravine. It was slow, tedious work, but gradually the bridge broke off chunks of the side of the ravine as it tumbled over the brink making the divide a few feet wider.

It wasn't an impossible jump—Porter had done wider over the San Rafael River when Matamoros's men were on his heels—but nobody here had witnessed that or there would have been bets on Port's life.

"Catching up to us ain't worth a broken neck," said Quincy.

"That's right. They might could try and make that jump, but I doubt it," said Porter, admiring his own handiwork.

"Can't they run east or west and find another spot to cross?"

"Sure, they can, and they will, but it will buy us more time. Let's get going."

They were almost over the next rise when they heard Shaw's curses billowing through the air. Porter looked back and tipped his hat, then crossed over the ridge.

3. Bad Wording

The second day on the trail and they rode into a familiar enough sight. Passing through Green River/Ferry-Town was odd now. More than half the population was gone; dead and buried in a lost canyon Port and the others had sworn never to return to. Luckily, one of those left in town had taken to repairing the ferry from its trouble and the damage Porter had done not more than two-weeks gone by.

They got some dirty looks from the remaining townsfolk and some appreciative ones too, well everyone except Redbone that is. There were too many hard feelings toward the Ute chieftain, but nobody was going to do anything about it either, at least not with Port and the others there. Instead the townsfolk glowered, frowned, and spat but otherwise kept their mouths closed.

Porter paid the toll, and they were soon crossing the roaring, torrential Green River.

"What about when Shaw gets here?" asked Roxy.

Porter shrugged. "I can only do so much. You got an idea?"

"Maybe." She drew a gold coin from her purse and showed it to the boy running the tug line. "This is for you if you wait on this side until a posse of men come wanting to cross after us. You go ahead and bring them across but you tell them we went south along the river. Got it?"

The boy eagerly nodded pocketing the coin.

They rode on south along the river until they were out of sight of the boy and the ferry, then they crossed a rocky ridge and went on east.

"Think that will fool Shaw? Cuz it won't," said Porter.

"Just buying time like you did."

"Good girl," said Port with a laugh.

On the other side, up above the river lowlands, a barren wilderness welcomed them like fire welcomes fuel. This would be among the worst of the landscapes they would have to traverse. There were no trees, no shade, and no shelter from the elements for at least twenty miles, just hard packed rolling hillocks with nary a blade of grass growing between the cracks. A more hellish landscape Porter couldn't imagine, but then he had grown up in New England, moved to Ohio, then Illinois and finally the Utah territories. Quite a difference. Not that he would change any of that, this was home now.

Redbone was sure he could pick up the trail. He said that Matamoros had attacked his village then headed back down toward the Old Spanish Trail. They would come across his trace soon enough.

"I cannot understand how he found our village," said Redbone, musing along the trail. It was the most he had spoken all day. "We were hidden in a narrow canyon. I cannot help but think we were sold out by someone."

"Who? Who could know your villages hidden place? Except us?" asked Quincy.

Redbone gave him an accusing scowl.

"Obviously, he came to us for help," broke in Roxy. "He knows we had nothing to do with it. Right, Redbone?"

Redbone said, "I have no answers, but am greatly troubled." There was silence along the trail a few moments.

Porter finally said, "Well, since Matamoros survived, he must have wanted to take out some revenge on somebody. I killed a bunch of his men—"

"We all did," said Quincy.

"Right, but I'm the one who really insulted him and freed his prisoners on the plain. Even some white women. He must have taken that pretty bad as an insult. Hell, and then he lost most anyone he had left back in the canyon, so what else is he gonna do but cut his losses, gain some more prisoners and head on south to lick his wounds and make a little scratch?"

Quincy was indignant. "Don't refer to people as scratch."

Porter shrugged and tipped his hat. "No offense was meant."

"I hear you, but remember they're people, Yankee."

Roxy asked, "Do you think he was just rounding up whoever he could then? Or did he have something specific in mind by taking those women and children?"

"Well, women and kids is easier to abduct and keep prisoner than the menfolk. More interested buyers for slaves like them too, I imagine."

"I imagine," said Quincy heatedly.

"Damnit, Quint, no offense. I'm just reasoning this out and denying that something took place isn't gonna help us solve it."

"I'm just asking you to remember they are people!"

"Well, hell, of course I haven't forgotten that! That's why we're here!"

"You two need to settle it down," commanded Roxy.

"I am afraid that I have brought a curse upon my people because the treasure was disturbed," Redbone wiped away a tear.

"No, its just life," said Roxy.

"I am responsible. That is why they took my daughter. Dark spirits are at work."

"Redbone," said Porter, putting a hand on the warrior's shoulder. "Trust me, Matamoros is not the tool of the Great Spirit to punish anyone. He is just a bad man, and we're all caught in the thick of it. Especially you in the here and now, but we're gonna do everything we can to make it right."

"I hear the spirits whispering to me that there is bad medicine involved," answered Redbone.

"Well, sure there is. A good person wouldn't do what Matamoros does, he's bound to be surrounded by bad spirits, and we're trailing him, so we hear their haunting words on the wind."

"I don't like thinking about this. Can we not talk about that side of things?" said Roxy, unconsciously drawing her shawl about herself a little tighter.

"I'm just telling it like it is, Little Sister."

"How about you stop talking and aggravating your friends," said Quincy.

"Fine," grumbled Port, throwing his left hand in the air and letting his horse trot a few paces ahead of the others.

❋❋❋

It was a long, hot ride and they were only too glad to come to a stop that evening in Crescent Junction. There was a small saloon, a few homesteads, and a handful of comforts but no beds. After rubbing down the horses and getting them some much needed water and grain, they prepared their own bedding for the night.

"Beginning to think I'll never have a good night's sleep," said Quincy, as he stretched out before the campfire.

"One fine day," Porter joked. "When you've got your own spread, buy the best one you can afford."

Quincy laughed. "Yeah, and it's funny because I've got enough gold now to buy this dump and then some, but I can't spend it since we're right back on the trail."

"Doing what we do best," said Porter, sliding his hat down over his eyes.

Roxy poked at the dying coals of their campfire with a long, thin willow branch. "What if we're too late? What if the trail is too cold? Redbone found us two days after all this happened and its now two days after that. Matamoros could be a week ahead of us since he could have cut right through the Swell, and we've gone around it to get to the Trail." She sighed heavily as if hoping for a response; some kind of comfort that only Port could offer her.

Porter didn't shift his hat or even move to respond. "You thinking we shouldn't even bother?"

"No," she said defensively, throwing her stick into the fire. "Just worried is all. That's a big head start on us."

"It is," Porter agreed. "But we also know which way he's going. We'll find the trail sure as shooting. Besides, having those prisoners is going to slow him down, so that's on our side too."

"I hadn't thought of that."

"Don't call 'em prisoners," Quincy interjected. "They are kidnapped victims bound for slavery or worse. Prisoners doesn't make it sound serious enough for my blood."

"Fine," grumbled Porter.

"I'm just saying," said Quincy.

"Kidnapped victims. You happy? Either way, we are getting them back and Matamoros is gonna pay in blood."

"I will cut out his heart," declared Redbone, from the edge of the darkness.

Porter grunted in the affirmative and turned over in his bedding. He was soon snoring.

**

The moon rolled out from behind a mountain of clouds and owls hooted ominously. Somewhere a dog barked and a whore cooed exuberantly from behind the saloon, and Roxy thought it was going to be the longest night of her life. She was anxious to get moving and deal out some justice. Then she realized there was someone even more restless than herself. Redbone remained off in the gloom, staring at the moonlit hills far to the south.

"Redbone. Are you going to be all right?" she asked.

His mask of stone began melting. "I'm afraid," he said. "Afraid, I'll never see her again." He dropped to his knees.

She clutched him to her chest. "We are going to help you. You will see her again. I swear it."

He composed himself and stood, wiping away a tear. "I am sorry for my weakness."

"It's all right," Roxy said. "We've all been there. Lost someone we loved and weren't sure what would happen. Trust me, we are going to see this through. We will get her back. Why don't you try and get some sleep?"

"I cannot sleep."

"You need to try. We all need our strength come morning. We have a long way to go, but we'll do it just the same."

He nodded, even though it didn't seem like he believed her.

They walked back to the camp and each lay down upon their bedrolls. Roxy was glad that between the dogs, owls, and whores the last had gone quiet.

Soon enough, she heard the steady rhythmic breathing of Redbone and knew he was asleep. Now if only she could follow her own advice.

4. Blood on the Sand

Morning came, or at least what she thought was morning. Roxy awoke to Porter kicking her toes. "Rise and shine, Little Sister, we gotta get moving. We're burning daylight."

It was still dark with just the faintest hint of a light turquoise scraping at the horizon.

"Now?" she asked, tired and comfortable in her bedroll.

"Now," Porter said. "We gotta cut all the time we can on Matamoros and break that gap."

"Do we have anything to eat?"

"I got a few vittles warmed up in the pan there, if you hurry. I want to be riding in the next ten minutes."

She nodded and rubbed the sleep from her eyes. Redbone was already awake and Quincy was too, rolling up his bedroll.

"Do we know where they are going?" she asked. "All this barren desert looks much the same to me. What's even out here?"

"A whole lot of nothing, but yeah I know. He's on the Old Spanish Trail. He'll be making his way toward Santa Fe and then on down south to old Mexico."

"How do you know?"

"This land is pretty inhospitable; the easiest routes have been found by explorers going back centuries, precious few places in this world someone hasn't been walking on. It's the route he'll take all right."

"I guess I just wanted to know how you could be so sure."

Porter laughed and said, "This ain't my first rodeo."

Roxy frowned, she knew all the stories of this ancient land. She didn't want to think about them anymore, because if she thought too long, she would have to face her past too. Grunting, she packed up, ready to hit the trail.

They moved down the trail like ghosts, silent, with moonlight nipping at their heels. As dawn came, the scenery changed from dull yellow browns, to stark red cliffs on all sides.

Redbone suddenly broke the stillness with a fierce cry. He raised an arm to signal a halt. "They are close, I can feel it."

"Maybe just over that rise?" asked Porter, as he tipped his hat back and wiped away the beading sweat.

Redbone nodded as he dismounted and crawled on his belly up the top of the next slope to peek over. It was plain that he was still fighting through the pain of his leg wound. He sprawled beside a spiny yucca bush to hide his outline. Then he dashed over the top, disappearing from view.

"That dad blamed fool!" cursed Porter, drawing his guns and spurring his horse. But just as suddenly Redbone appeared at the peak again shouting in glee.

Redbone babbled excitedly in Ute, pointing at the ground.

Porter rubbed at his beard and took a swallow of Valley-Tan. Maybe this trip would be over a whole lot quicker than anyone figured.

"What is it?" asked Roxy.

"He found the trail, he's sure of it," answered Porter. "He can tell by the moccasins of the children being drug along. We're in luck."

"How?"

"He says these tracks can't be more than a few hours old. They are going a little slow. We hurry and we can catch them by noon!"

They cantered their horses, picking up the pace while still not running their mounts ragged. The red, rocky ground was treacherous enough without that worry.

In less than a mile, Porter thought he heard a child's terrible wail in the distance. It was beyond pain and fear, it was sheer tormented terror, and it tugged at his heart as strong as anything.

Evil had happened over that rise and a child had endured something no one should.

"Is that a child?" asked Roxy.

"Sure, sounds like it," said Quincy.

Redbone was almost uncontrollable and raced ahead.

"Hold on!" cried Porter. "We don't want to ride face first into any traps. Let's take it easy, for all our sakes."

Redbone wheeled his horse around, glaring. "It is my daughter!"

"I know, but it won't do anyone any good to ride into a trap. Matamoros is deadlier than a rattler, we've got to be careful. Everyone, have your guns loaded and loose. We might start throwing lead in a hurry."

They edged closer, ever wary of any hiding spots a gun barrel might be pointing from toward them.

A few hundred yards away, they all heard the young girl's terrible cries. She was whimpering now, as if the fight had left her. She was dying, and Porter knew it before he even saw her.

Alone in the world, the wounded child cried out pitifully when she heard their approach. One last call for help. One last call for relief.

Redbone leapt from his horse and hit his knees at the ground beside her.

Roxy gasped and looked away. Quincy took off his hat.

What they saw was shocking. A young girl, maybe eight years old, was lying in a pool of her own blood. She had been horribly maimed by the wretched slavers. Her limbs were completely severed at the elbows and knees and her eyes gouged out.

Redbone was beside himself, tearing at the red sands in agony.

The girl went silent.

Redbone screamed aloud, casting sand over himself while howling.

"I'm so sorry," said Roxy, as she blanched and turned away.

Quincy took off his hat and put it over his heart. "We'll make them pay."

"Count on it," Porter growled.

"Do you want to bury her?" asked Roxy, putting a hand on his shoulder.

They waited while Redbone composed himself, managing to speak. "She was not my daughter. But I knew her. Her name was Lozen. She was a trouble maker, but did not deserve this. They wanted to make an example of her."

Porter dismounted and stared shoveling sand.

"We have no time for that," said Redbone. "We must hurry."

"You hurry, I'm gonna bury this little girl you were just crying over," growled Porter.

"It breaks my heart to see her," whispered Redbone.

"Me too, me too."

They buried the girl in a shallow grave, and then stacked rocks over the top to keep the coyotes and vultures off. Porter said a quick prayer and Quincy gave a loud amen. Redbone and Roxy remained silent. It took only a few minutes, less than they might have wished to spend, and they were back on the trail.

They kept as swift a pace as Porter would allow, being cautious every time they came around a bend in the hills or crested one of the rolling rocky slopes. It wouldn't do to rush headlong into Matamoros and the slavers unprepared. Last thing they needed was to be ambushed.

Just as they were near the top of some sweeping dunes, Porter made them stop again.

Roxy especially appreciated the stop as she needed a long drink of water. She dismounted and stretched her aching legs. Quincy jumped down and ran off behind a bush, only because Roxy was present.

Redbone, on the other hand, almost jumped out of his skin in excitement. He turned around and signaled, let's go. He ran back to his horse and kicked its flanks to race over the crest.

"Wait! You damn fool!" cried Porter.

Roxy was left watching as the two of them vanished over the top of the red hill.

Quincy peered out from around a juniper bush. "What?"

"Let's get after them!" hollered Roxy. She cursed, as struggled to clamber back on her horse. Being horribly saddle-sore wasn't going to keep her from the fight. It didn't help that she had a terribly sick feeling in the pit of her stomach after witnessing what had been done to the child.

Quincy had time to mount up and start out after Porter and Redbone. He pulled his buffalo gun out of its scabbard and made ready for a fight.

Below the ridge, there were a string of women and children being led by a dozen horsemen. They stopped cold soon as they saw the riders coming.

Redbone had a good lead on Porter. He kicked his horse to top speed, running straight at the Matamoros, his Apache henchmen and his daughter.

Matamoros, still dressed in his fancy black outfit with silver bells and Spanish accruements, though it was now dirty, faded, and scuffed. "Kill them! Shoot! Shoot!" He drew his six-gun and began shooting at the oncoming riders. At first, he felt nothing but irritation when he saw the two men cresting the hill, but when he saw two more after that, his sense of panic rose. Sure, that there must be a train of men coming after him. He fired his six rounds at them, then lunged for what he deemed was his prize slave, a raven-haired girl of perhaps thirteen.

He grabbed the girl, despite her violent protests, and struck her across the face and neck until she went limp. He strung her over his saddle and took off riding hard.

Redbone rode straight at Matamoros, his Sharps rifle in one hand, reins and trigger in the other. He fired precisely at the Apache so he would not hit the prisoners. He hit one and yelled with glee to see the red bandana and skull beneath it explode with his bullet.

They fired back, missing their incoming target, who was whooping like the devil.

Porter wasn't too far behind, shielding Redbone and keeping their heads down with his own thunderous Navy Colt.

But then the Apache hit Redbone's horse. It screamed and tumbled end over end. Redbone was thrown to the earth, lucky he wasn't crushed by the reeling animal. A cloud of dust erupted, giving a scant amount of cover for him behind the dead horse.

Porter swooped in behind him, but wasn't about to let his horse be a target. He dropped down beside Redbone, urged his horse away and ducked against the dead horse as cover.

The stallion instinctively ran back the way it had come, away from the flying lead. Porter took careful aim with both of his Navy Colts and dispatched an Apache rifleman with deadly accuracy.

Porter noticed a sizeable difference between white women he had rescued a couple weeks ago and the Utes. The Ute hostages didn't scream and cry out during the gunfight. They bided their time and when the moment struck, wrapped their bonds about their captors to strangle the life out of them.

One of the Apache's was pulled down and pummeled to death by the squaws, but three more fought their way free of the enraged captives. They gained their horses and left in a mad dash after Matamoros.

Another was trapped by the revenge minded Ute's and kept them back swinging his rifle. He killed three, but that gave Porter time to close the distance and put a bullet through his brain. Smoke from Porter's Navy Colt encircled him like a devilish halo.

Two more braves ran to their horses, sensing they had lost this fight with their leader already fled.

Quincy stopped and dismounted so he could have a rock steady perch.

Porter took aim and blasted one as he was mounting his horse. The man flew over top of the panicked beast and hit the rocks with a sickening crunch.

Quincy got the other one from a spectacularly good distance. He taunted the rest as they fled. This caused one of the Apache to turn in the saddle and send a bullet frighteningly close. The bullet ricocheted off a rock less than a foot from Quincy's head. But this only made him laugh in triumph as he shot at them again before they vanished over the hill.

Roxy stopped to see to Redbone.

He was already struggling to his feet and stumbling toward the women and children.

"Kimama," cried Redbone. "Where is she?"

One of the squaws pointed in the direction of the fleeing riders.

Redbone seized the reins of one of the horses left by the Apache and struggled to mount it. He fumbled with the stirrups and finally succeeded in getting on, only to be bucked off by a mount that knew he was not its master. This time he didn't get up right away but lay upon the ground gasping for air.

Quincy examined him and pronounced, "He has a concussion. He has got to rest."

Porter spat, "Damn it, but we were close too! Almost had him, and now he ain't got to slow down for a bunch women and kids."

Roxy was back on her horse, "Let's get going then."

Quincy agreed, "We can catch them Porter, let's go."

Redbone coughed and tried to stand but fell back down, delirious.

Porter shook his head. "No, we whittled 'em down real good but Redbone has got to do this. We are just support."

"You sure? We can get 'em."

Porter was adamant. "No. Right now we could run right into a guarded spot with good cover for them and a death trap for us. They're hurting, they're spooked. We got 'em between a rock and the Colorado River. We got 'em, we just gotta be patient and not make any fool decisions."

"I hope you know what you're doing," said Roxy.

"I do. Redbone must be the one to save his daughter. Otherwise he'll lose face with his tribe. That is, unless they kill him and they damn near did."

Neither Quincy nor Roxy liked that, but they agreed and it was plain to see that Redbone needed some help recuperating.

"I don't like it though, we know they are close," said Quincy.

Porter said, pointing in a southerly direction. "We got them trapped. The way they are going is going to get them stuck against the cliffs above the Colorado. There's no way down. We can take the time."

One of the old squaws made a poultice from plants nearby and took to caring for the delirious chief. They made camp for the evening with Porter or Quincy keeping a good eye out for Matamoros and his men, just in case they doubled back.

A lone coyote gave a howl and it was a happy evening for those that had been rescued but bittersweet for Redbone once he came to.

"We'll follow their trail in the morning. We'll get 'em. No worries about that. Soon enough this will all be 'Wheat in the mill'," said Porter.

5. Nightmares

Roxy woke from a nightmare to the sound of voices, soft and fearful. The squaws were speaking with Redbone in hushed whispers.

Redbone listened stoically, only occasionally responding with a word or two in adamant opposition to what the women urged.

Roxy couldn't understand what they said, but she could understand the fear sure enough. Something in said the conversation made her blood run cold though she had no idea why. What were they talking about?

After a time, the women went quiet and lay down to sleep. Redbone on the other hand got up and strode away into the gloom.

Roxy followed.

He sat upon a ledge of rock pointing at the moon.

"Redbone? Tell me what that was all about. What did they tell you that brought so much fear? Are they afraid that Matamoros will come back?"

"No," he said.

"What then?"

"You should not worry. It is the talk of old women."

"I know you're lying. You aren't any good at it."

"It is not good to say. It invites evil."

Roxy stared at the sleeping camp. "We are friends. You need to let us know what we're up against. We are here to help you. You can't let us walk into anything blind. What were they telling you?"

"What I say is for the circle only. I am afraid. The women tell me Matamoros is afraid."

Redbone stood up and drew a circle in the dirt around them, while chanting in a low hushed tone. He then burned a small bundle of sage and waved its smoke all about them.

"Him? Of what? Us?"

Redbone shook his head. "He does not fear men, not me or my Blood Brother. He fears the dark, the spirits that call and command. One has called for him and demands sacrifice. It tells him he must bring my daughter to him or he will die."

Roxy tried to make sense of the words. "Spirits can't do that. What do you mean."

Redbone scowled at her. "Just because you cannot understand a thing does not mean it is not so."

"I'm sorry. Forgive me. Please tell me again. We are still in the magic circle," she prodded.

Redbone nodded at her logic. "A dark spirit calls for blood of the innocent. The girl, Lozen, was left as a sacrifice to the dark powers."

"Are you saying she wasn't just tortured, but was part of some witchcraft?"

Redbone nodded. "He wants my daughter and other innocents. If Matamoros does not bring him blood, he will kill him. Matamoros will stop at nothing to deliver."

"Who is this dark spirit? What do you mean by that?"

Redbone searched for a way to say what he meant. "Old, very old, black magic haunts this land. Witches call here and demand sacrifice. Is a bad thing. I fear one of us will die to bring my daughter home. If it has to be anyone, it should be me."

"No. I won't let that happen."

He smiled and put a hand on her shoulder. "It is not your call."

6. On the Midnight Trail

Shaw led his posse over the rough, yellow ground til it turned red. He was a good enough tracker he had no problem following Porter's trail no matter what the Mormon gunslinger had done to try and confuse him. It was almost dusk when they came upon a small cairn of stones.

"What in tarnation is that?" asked his deputy, Matty. He scratched at his belly a moment before quenching his thirst.

"Don't know yet," said Shaw, as he dismounted. "There's a fair amount of blood on the ground nearby though." He examined the crimson earth. Patches of dark purple were spilled here and there. "Someone bled out here. There too much for anyone to have lived."

"You sure it's a person and not game?"

"I'm sure. This is a burial."

"Who? Should we open it up?" asked Matty.

Shaw pondered. He hated the idea of defiling the dead, but he needed answers.

"That's desecration," argued one of the others.

"Yes, it is, but were looking for evidence to convict that worst killer in the west, and we must leave no stone unturned. Open her up."

The posse got to work removing the stones and scooping back sand until they discovered the horrid state of the body.

"Dear Lord in heaven!" exclaimed Matty. "You think Porter did this?"

"He did. It must be some kind of sick joke to keep slowing us down," said Shaw.

"What do you think? Do we just add it to the list of his crimes?"

"Yes. But bury her back up. We aren't keeping a body like that as evidence, I'll not be called a Levite cutting up his concubine for my justice in Mormon lands."

"Huh?" asked a deputy.

"Judges 19," answered Matty.

"Who is that?"

Matty huffed in exasperation with his partner. "You call yourself a Bible reading Christian?"

The slack-jawed deputy thought a moment then responded, "No, not really."

"You ought to be in this god-forsaken country."

"Enough!" shouted Shaw. "We're all witnesses and that's evidence enough. We'll keep on Porter's trail and get more answers. He can't out run justice forever."

"It's getting awful dark, Boss," said Matty. "I got my doubts on following a Midnight Trail."

Shaw nodded without answering. With every moment lost he knew Porter was still moving, pushing his people hard to elude justice. But what was out here? Shaw knew just enough about the area to reckon what a death trap it was. What if that's what this was? A trap for him. "We had better wait 'til morning for some amount of light. But we aren't staying near this corpse. We'll move on a little and run a cold camp."

They mounted up and went another quarter mile in the dark before stopping for the night.

7. Red Lands

In the early morning, Redbone bid the women and children to make their way back to their own clan's territory. He spoke in hushed whispers to them, to Porter and the others it sounded like he didn't think he would come back at all. If he couldn't rescue his daughter, he would die in the attempt.

To these instructions, the women and children agreed without complaint or question. They bid him and the others farewell beginning their journey back to their tribal grounds.

Matamoros's trail was easy to follow. The sandy ground betrayed his every move. They followed the trail through stark canyons and tall towering monuments of red rock, many with wondrous designs and features to be found nowhere else on earth. In one spot, there were no less than three great arches of stone, vaulting out of the rusty hills. Roxy had never seen such a beautiful piece of nature, but remembering Redbone's words in the night gave her pause. She rode up beside Porter to talk to him. She watched to see that Redbone did not notice.

"Porter?"

"Yeah?"

"Redbone told me some things last night that he learned from the squaws."

"What? Why didn't he tell me?"

"Well, he drew a magic circle around us before he told me. Said it was sacred and had to be repeated there where it was safe, I guess."

"Then maybe you shouldn't be telling me outside the circle," he said, with a laugh.

She looked puzzled. "I can't tell if you are serious or not."

"I am serious. I've seen a lot of things ain't nobody gonna ever be able to explain, but yeah tell me. What did he say?"

"He said the girl was a sacrifice to dark magics. That there are bad spirits that want us dead and I guess Matamoros is afraid and supposed to deliver the girl to . . . well, something."

Porter wiped at his mouth, then rubbed his chin, like he always did when he was thinking.

"Well?"

"Well, what?"

"I thought you'd have an answer."

"Me?"

"Yes you."

He laughed out loud, making Redbone look back at him. "No, I don't have any answers, but I can't say I'm surprised there isn't something like that attached to this. I've seen some strange things in my time and this is just another one. We got to make our own way in this world and keep strong."

"He was afraid it would invite doom on us. That one of us would die getting the girl back."

"Anything is possible."

"That's not helping."

"I am helping. I'm saying we can't worry about that crap. We just gotta do the right thing and trust in the Lord that we'll be all right."

"That's pretty easy talk from a man who was blessed that no bullet nor blade can harm him."

A great gust of wind came up with her words and she had to wonder at it.

Port gave a chuckle before answering, "Trust me, Little Sister, there's plenty other ways to die out here and when it's your time—it's your time. But living with the fear of it won't help anybody." He gave spurs to his horse and trotted ahead to Redbone, saying, "Don't scare the Lucky Woman no more."

Redbone glowered at Roxy, his eyes flashing.

"Damnit, Porter, you ruined our bond!" cried Roxy.

Porter shrugged.

"I finally had a bond of trust with him," she grumbled.

The trail continued almost due south, six horsemen moving together like a murder of crows, flitting one way and then the other across the rocky, rough ground.

They found the camp Matamoros had used in the night and one Apache lay there dead. He must have been wounded in the gunfight and left to die. He had been picked clean by his companions left with no knife, ammunition, or anything else of value.

"They still heading to the river?" asked Quincy.

"Yeah. They'll need water just as bad as we do. But this route is crazy. We're heading straight to a sheer cliff face overlooking the river. I'm surprised he's painting himself into a corner."

"What if he has a secret way down to the river?"

"They'll still have to swim a helluva torrent; I expect we'll have 'em somewhere along the bank."

Sure enough, despite Matamoros trying to conceal his trail, they found his route down a notch in a gulley, leading to a red escarpment and down to the mighty Colorado River.

"This will be tough. We better dismount and lead the horses down."

It was a precarious ride, leading their horses down over the broken bits of shale and flint. Once a horse nearly slid over the side and would have surely been killed, but Porter held onto the reins while Redbone and Quincy pushed her back.

An hour later, they were finally down to a rolling, sagebrush covered hillside. It was the only place in the canyon they could have possibly come down as near as Porter could tell. The river's edge was thick with tamarisk, but Porter still found a sandy shoreline with prints went that right up to the river, there was some milling about and then all six sets of tracks went into the water.

"They must have had the horses swim across," said Porter.

"That risky?" asked Quincy.

"It's nothing I would do if I didn't have to."

"But we do have to," said Roxy, sending her horse into the brown, flowing murk.

"Everybody keep your eyes peeled, in case they're waiting to ambush us in those tamarisk as we're crossing. Roxy! Maybe you ought to let me go first!"

She didn't stop but waved for him to follow.

"Hell! Cover us, Quint!" Porter raced his stallion into the river and was soon right beside Roxy. He half expected a shower of lead to come calling but it didn't. There was nothing, but the even dull roar of the river.

Quint and Redbone followed, splashing into the mirk.

They were swept down a good quarter mile in the effort to cross but had no troubles beyond that.

But there was another mystery. Once they crossed the Colorado River, the trail went cold as the grave.

8. The Mission

"They were right on the other side of the river, where did they go? They couldn't have landed any farther upriver than we did but I can't see any tracks!" Roxy shouted in exasperation. She spurred her horse to run farther down the bank.

"Wait," cried Porter. But, she was already a hundred yards downstream and still moving at a good clip. "You ain't gonna find anything!" He shouted.

"Whatchoo yelling about Port?" asked Quincy, as he came riding out of the river. Redbone followed close behind leading the pack horse.

"Simple. There's no tracks, right here where there should be, and Roxy is still running downstream because she hasn't seen anything either, then the answer is obvious. Matamoros is on a boat."

"Aw hell! You think he's riding the river?"

Redbone stood ankle deep in the river, looking downstream.

"I would." Porter said, as he signaled them to follow him. They rode upriver a few hundred yards and on the far side of the tamarisks they found the remains of an old camp. It had seen use for some time, judging by the trash pile and smelly remnants. "They had a flatboat here and looks like at least two more men, who had been left to watch and wait."

"Why haven't we heard anything about this before?"

"Who would we have asked?"

"Where are we gonna get a boat?"

Porter shrugged in the saddle. "Not here. We keep moving on downriver, talk to the folks at the Mission and see if they've seen anybody going past. Maybe they'll even have a ferry we can borrow, cause I sure ain't gonna risk losing the horses."

Redbone flinched when Porter said Mission, but then he returned to his usual somber scowl.

Quincy shook his head and stretched his arm out, pointing at the mighty Colorado. "That's a hell of a gamble, Porter. What if they just went a mile downstream and got off again?"

"Well then we'll see their tracks, won't we? 'Sides, trust me, there ain't nowhere they're gonna land on the opposite bank. Cliffs are too high for a good stretch. We'll find the trail even if it is in the river."

Roxy finally turned her mount around and was racing back toward them.

"Look at that, she's more fired up than Redbone," said Quincy, under his breath to Porter. "Gotta admire a woman with so much fire in her belly."

Porter grunted in the affirmative.

Roxy brought her horse to a sudden halt before them. "I don't see any sign of them. Nothing. What do you think? A ferry?"

"Had to be," said Porter. "Now we gotta see about getting our own. Let's get moving."

They rode together in grim silence a couple miles down through a winding canyon upon sandy, rock-strewn banks. One offshoot canyon had grassy fields and cattle grazed lazily in the cool afternoon.

Redbone seemed surprised to see the cattle. None of this was lost on Porter, but he didn't say anything. They rounded the bend to a wide valley. Not too far distant they saw the stone blocks of the Elk Mountain mission. It looked like a fortress.

"There she is. I haven't been here in quite a spell," said Porter.

"Wait, my brother. I need to tell you," said Redbone.

"What is it?"

"We chased out the settlers here."

"When?" asked Porter, none too surprised at Redbone's revelation considering his curious behavior since the river crossing.

"One moon ago. There were disagreements between my people and those at the fort. There was shooting and some were killed."

"How many?" Porter asked, frowning.

Redbone shook his head. "I don't know. Your people left, abandoning the fort and some cattle. I thought there would be no more."

"Maybe they came back?" suggested Quincy.

Redbone shrugged. "They told us they would not return." But smoke rose from the chimney of the fort.

"Somebody's in there," said Porter.

"You think it could be Matamoros?" asked Roxy.

Porter shook his head. "I wouldn't think he would stop so close to Ute territory. He's gotta know there will be repercussions for what he did. Unlessen he thought all of your clan was wiped out and he could rest a day or two?"

Redbone's face darkened, "He killed many of my clan."

"Uh huh," Porter grunted angrily. "And how many of mine did you butcher in these parts?"

Roxy put her hand on Port's shoulder, "Please. This won't help."

Quincy glanced back and forth between the two.

"I want a straight answer, Blood Brother. Especially since I'm putting my own neck and these other folks on the line for you. You owe me that much."

Redbone shook his head. "I took cattle for my people. We took squash. When arguments came, I was not here. I know both my people and yours killed each other, until yours chose to leave. We had a great feast in celebration. This land was ours alone again." He paused a long moment then said, "My uncle, Chief St. John, felt guilty for the feuding and he returned many cattle to yours as they were departing across the river. That is why I didn't think to see cattle here."

Porter grimaced, but said, "All right. But I've got to have your word that you and yours will leave my people alone unless you're defending your own lives."

"You ask a hard thing."

"You bet I do, but I can't be turning a blind eye to your running off settlers."

Redbone's gaze was hard as stone once again.

"Your word." Porter demanded, extending his hand.

Redbone stared at the calloused hand a long moment. Then took it in a firm shake.

"I still aim to get your daughter back, and settle with Matamoros once and for all. I can't imagine he would have had any cattle, even if he had some men in reserve upriver."

"But?" asked Quincy.

"We can't take any chances. We go in ready for bear." Porter checked his guns were fully loaded, including a shot gun.

"We leave the horses here with Roxy, and the three of us creep up on the fort."

"Hey, I can shoot."

"Yeah, but I don't want you getting shot. And its best to have some back up. That's you. With the horses," he said, leaving no room for argument.

The men snaked their way over some short dunes, always keeping their eyes on the fort. One advantage, as Port saw it, was that even in broad daylight there were no windows so no one could be looking out and just see them. They kept their eyes trained for any movement, any sign of a watchman upon the walls. Nothing.

Smoke still trailed out of a chimney, denoting a cookfire. A few chickens and a few more cattle milled about nearby. There was no longer a garden of any kind as Redbone had said, the Utes had taken everything edible that grew.

They slowly traced their way around to the front of the fort. Its walls were twelve feet high, and it was at least five times that long. Still no sign of life alerted them as to who could be inside. The big thick doors hung open. There were a few bullet holes in the doors and traces of sand bleeding from those wounds.

Circling around front, a few short aspen trees caught the wind and fluttered, their bright green leaves shaking back and forth. They paused, scanning in every direction for any sign of life. The smell of an apple pie baking drifted out of the open fort doors to them.

"Smells good," whispered Porter.

"What if it's a trap?" asked Quincy.

"Then it's a damn good one. I'll go first," said Porter, as he sprinted toward the wall. He put his back to it and glanced back the way he had come and beyond. Scrutinizing in case there were enemies farther out beyond the rocky slopes.

Quincy shook his head and watched up toward the top of the wall. He expected shots to ring out, but all was still save the sound of the leaves being tossed by the wind. That apple pie sure did smell good.

He took a deep breath and ran at the wall beside Porter, expecting a sniper would shoot him once he saw there were more men coming. But, silence met his ears.

Redbone made the sprint next, faster than both civilized men. His rifle was ready, but there was no sign of anything amiss.

Still watching every conceivable direction, they slowly made their way through breach. Porter was first, then Quincy and finally Redbone, watching behind them as they moved like one body inside.

They heard whistling and a young blonde woman came through the doors on the side of the fort. She had a line stretched for laundry and began hanging clothing to dry.

Porter recognized her as one of several he had rescued from Matamoros only a week ago.

He whistled to her.

She turned in shock and fear then in grateful surprise. "Mr. Rockwell! Am I glad to see you! I never got to thank you enough."

"Ma'am," Porter said, tipping his hat. He had no idea what her name was. "Looks like you and yours made it here all right then?"

"Well, it wasn't without difficulty, but we made it here a few days ago."

"Anybody else here? I only just heard the Mission got abandoned."

"Was abandoned," corrected a man from a side door. He was a big black man, wearing buckskins and a bent ten-gallon hat. He had a long Sharps rifle leaning on the doorframe at his side, but he was holding a plate with a slice of pie. "You must be Orrin Porter Rockwell, heard a lot about you just lately. I'm Bill Granstaff. Some folks call me Negro Bill and some others call me Nigger Bill."

"Do they now?" asked Quincy, with a smirk.

"Some," said Bill, with a laugh. "Some say a whole lot worse."

"Ahem," came another male voice from behind him. This was a very tall man wearing a beaver hat. He had a scruffy face and a bushy, black mustache.

"And that's Frenchie. We both settled in here a couple weeks ago. Seemed a shame to not use it, since the place was abandoned."

"Oui," said Frenchie.

"Then these sweet little ladies happened by, said you told them to come here?" Bill gestured with his fork. Then took another bite of pie.

"I did. Course at the time I was hip-deep in trouble with the slaver, Matamoros, and some other pukes."

Bill squinted, like he thought he had caught Porter in a lie, but nodded saying, "I suppose I understand. Just the three of you?"

Porter shook his head. "No, a friend has our horses. We weren't sure what to expect since my friend, Redbone here, said the settlers were chased out recently."

"The Chief Redbone?" Bill laughed. "Didn't he help chase 'em off?"

Porter glanced at Redbone with a scowl but didn't say anything to contest the accusation.

Bill continued anyway. "My, you do have an interesting collection of friends, yes sir," Bill extended a hand toward Quincy. "And who are you?"

They shook hands. "I'm Quincy Cuthbert Jackson. I was with the—,"

"Save it," said Bill, breaking the shake. "We're all just doing the best we can out here, titles don't mean a thing."

Porter could see that burned Quincy, he was awful proud of serving with distinction in the Union Army, the Buffalo soldiers and just lately helping take down the Cotterell Gang and the Thorn/Mort outfit, even if he couldn't brag about that last part.

"Who else you got out there?" asked Bill.

"Roxy Lejeune. Redbone, why don't you have her come on in with the horses?" said Porter. Redbone vanished.

"A woman? You do have an interesting posse, now don't you?"

"Posse?" asked Porter.

"And what makes everything so 'interesting'?" asked Quincy.

Porter put a hand on Quincy, since he knew he was getting riled. "This ain't an official posse sure, but we are after someone."

"Matamoros?" asked Bill.

"That's right. Speaking of which, you seen him come by here lately?"

"As a matter of fact, we did. That guy is a jackass. He rounded the bend in the river earlier today. Him and a couple of his Mexicans, hollered at us from their flat boat and even took a couple of pot-shots at us."

"Just Mexican's?" questioned Porter.

"He had a few Apache with him too. We returned the same, but nothing come if it. They kept floating downriver. Me and Frenchie even followed 'em down a spell just to be sure they didn't land and double back on us. But they didn't, they just a kept on a keeping on."

"How early today?"

"Midday. But, I sure don't think they stopped. They seemed in an awful hurry. That's on account of you all on their heels I take it."

"That'd be the size of it," said Porter.

"Well, why don't you get something to eat? Then I suppose you can move on after them in the morning," offered Bill.

"Much obliged. You got a ferry maybe we could borrow?"

Bill's face went from friendly to irritated in a flash. "Borrow? Let's just call a spade a spade, huh? Nobody is bringing no ferry back up that river, no how, no sir."

"Fine. You got a ferry to sell?"

"I've got one, but I ain't about to sell it. I need it when I ferry my cows across the river for their grazing. I can't get enough grass on this side. I take 'em over there and then back here every few days so there is time for each small patch to grow back. But uh-uh, I ain't selling."

"Easy brother," said Quincy. "It's important that we bring those men to justice."

"Who are you again? Just some lapdog, Uncle Tom? They deputize you and you think you're something special now?"

"Hey!"

"That's what I thought, just another Uncle Tom doing the work of the white man. Well, not out here you ain't. We got to look after ourselves out here, Tom."

Quincy cocked his head in a grin, and suddenly lashed out at Bill. The two exchanged hard blows as Porter and Frenchie moved to separate them.

Frenchie muttered, "Non, non, mon ami."

They got the two men to back away from each other, even if they were still staring daggers and breathing heavy.

"This ain't gonna help anyone," said Porter.

"Oui," agreed Frenchie.

"Look Bill, you got any other alternative you can offer me? I need to get after Matamoros. He's kidnapped some children, not unlike what he attempted with," Porter realized he still didn't know the blond girl or her mother's names, "them."

The woman smiled at Porter and said, "I'm Mae Taggart. And I wanted to thank you again."

Her daughter, who had been hanging laundry, gave the prettiest smile and said, "I'm Emily, these are my sisters Tana, Jean, and Flora."

Porter tipped his hat, "Ma'am. Misses."

Quincy jerked free of Porter and strode out the fort doors. Roxy, who had just entered with the horses, saw Quincy seething and promptly followed him.

"Your man has got a temper," said Bill.

"You riled him."

"Entendons nous."

"We are getting along, Frenchie. I just ain't agreeing to giving them my ferry so they can do a fool chase after a killer they won't ever catch, or if they do, he'll kill them, and I'll still be out a ferry!"

Porter grimaced. "I can pay you for the damn ferry."

"What good is that gonna do me on my day to day business out here? Huh? I take care of myself, I take care of my cows and thanks to you telling them to come here, now I'm taking care of five white ladies. Hell, if someone less discriminating in his friends than you were to show up, I'd probably get hung for this."

Mae looked away and Emily blushed. "We probably ought to be getting moving along. We haven't meant to cause you any distress, Mr. Granstaff."

Bill wiped at his forehead, "I'm sorry for what I said, you ladies are not inconveniencing me. I'm just worried about what other folks might say. I don't ever want to get chased out of this valley. It's my home now and forever I hope."

"Oh Bill, we really haven't meant to be a bother."

Bill put up his hands like she had the drop on him. "No, no. It's been my pleasure having some lovely female company around."

"Bill," interrupted Porter. "I can pay you a lot for the ferry, a lot. How about for the next time that you do head on over to some kind of civilization, or Hell, even if you barter with someone else that is just passing through."

Bill frowned. "How about we think about it tonight over a bottle of that whiskey you have clinking in those saddle bags?"

Now it was Porter's turn to frown. He didn't want to give up any of his Valley-Tan for what he was afraid could turn into a long journey. But he knew he had to make sacrifices if he was going to expect anybody else too. "I can open one up for tonight and we can talk about more for a trade."

"My answer is still going to be no, unless you have another train of horses all carrying whiskey. So, unless you do, I don't expect you've got enough for it to be worth my while to lose my flatboat." Porter grimaced. He didn't want to share any whiskey with the man now, but they were getting some amount of hospitality, so he felt he still had to be accommodating.

9. Signs

The land was downright inhospitable. It baked you in the day and froze you in the evening. The wind slapped you in the face and spit dust in your gaping mouth. Dealing with the insulting weather, Shaw lost the trail, though he didn't admit it to his men for more than an hour. He made like he was hunting for shelter from the threatening gusts. Truth be told he lost the sign when the parties, Porter's and whomever he was trailing, went over some slick rock. On a good day, you could still track a man judging by the dust left near invisible, but in this storm and dim light that wasn't happening.

"Boss? What do you think?" asked Matty.

Shaw tipped his hat and stared at the horizon. "They gotta be heading to the river, but how they'll get off this mesa without doubling back is beyond me."

"You saying, we should wait them out?"

Shaw was kneeling, examining what may or may not have been a hoofprint in the shifting sands. "Maybe. That would be safer than walking into a trap. I don't think Porter is with friends at all. Whoever he is trailing after is a murderer too, and maybe they'll bust heads before we find 'em."

"That would be safest, Boss."

"Yep, horses are safest in the corral, but that isn't what horses are for, is it?"

"Boss?"

Shaw stood, directing the posse to keep going due south. "Our aim isn't to be safe. We got to bring some justice to this land."

They rode on, doing their damndest to ignore the pelting sand and the dryness of their tongues. When they came to the wide gorge they knew they were in trouble. It was late afternoon and they were no closer to the water. The red canyons held the teasing river at the bottom of a very high drop. Sunlight sprinkled across the dazzling brown surface, and the thirsty men's mouths salivated for that freshness.

In the near distance, they could see the beginnings of the Elk Valley opening. Maybe, just maybe Shaw could even see a wisp of smoke rising from just a little farther around the bend. They were so close and yet so far.

"Where could they have gone, Boss?"

"See that smoke? They are less than a mile from where we are now."

"How are we gonna get there, Boss?"

Shaw looked about. There was no possible route down from where they stood other than the sure death of straight down drop.

"They made it down, we must find their trail. Let's keep going."

They rode along the cliffs until they saw a lower spot of sage brush-covered hills gently lowering to the river. They couldn't make it down to those soft hills from where they were at all, the cliffs were still far too high, but Shaw figured they had to double back and find the beginning of a gulch or ravine that fed into the back of the egress. This took them another two hours to find and by then it was dusk, but they made it to the river.

"They must have crossed, huh? They just keep getting farther and farther ahead of us, huh?"

"Matty, I've had about enough of your observations. Keep it to yourself," grumbled Shaw. "Someone gather some firewood."

Shaw knew Porter and his men weren't on this side of the river, there was nowhere they could hide. This would make a decent enough camp for the evening and they would cross tomorrow.

Then the thought struck him. Porter wasn't even that far ahead along the opposite side of the river. He had seen the smoke of a campfire just a couple more miles down the river in the valley. Everyone was dog tired and the horses were sweating 'til salt showed on their flanks but if he got the men to show some gumption and cross, they should be able to overtake Porter in Elk Valley, not far along the bend of the river.

"We are gonna rest, eat some vittles, rub down the horses and cross the river."

"Boss?"

"Listen, we will catch up the them tonight and take Porter into custody based on the evidence of that befouled little girl."

"For all we know, he is the one that buried her," said one of the deputies.

Shaw snarled at him. "I'll see Porter hang for any reason I can get. Brew up some coffee. We are gonna cross in an hour."

Matty gulped at the prospect of a river crossing in the dark, especially one so wide as the Colorado, but he sure wasn't gonna go against Shaw either. "I'm on it, Boss."

10. A Day Late

Everyone seemed to deliberately avoid the pressing matters of earlier in the day, as they all sat making small talk around the fire pit. The settlers that had originally built the fort had worked to beautify the insides, planting a few small trees, growing flowers, and white washing the interior walls. Fine work had been done on the inside doors and there were even a few glass windows. A wooden parapet ran the entire rectangular distance about the fort at about nine feet in height. There were two steep, ladder-like stairways to climb up. All in all, it was a handsome set-up and Porter wondered at how bad the people who had built it must have felt to abandon it.

"You give any thought on if the folks that built this come back?" Porter asked.

Bill laughed. "Yes, sir. I talked with your Mormon Bishop that built it. He done signed over the rights. Said he wasn't ever coming back. The Utes killed his son don't you know? Bad memories here, he said. Between you and me I think he was having a crisis of faith and wasn't too sure about your golden bible and all its precepts and heeding Brigham's almighty word anymore."

"You trying to rile me?"

"No sir, I'm not. I don't think I'd want to rile the deadly Mormon triggerite that is Porter Rockwell, no sir."

"Please, don't," said Roxy.

"And who might you be miss?" asked Bill. He looked Roxy up and down in an appreciative manner.

But she didn't appreciate it. "I'm Roxy Lejeune, as if that's any business of yours."

"Well, it is since you all are staying in my place. I'm just trying to be friendly is all."

"The hell you say," muttered Quincy.

Mae Taggart worked to bring the peace. "I know we've all had our differences. I too had heard many a bloody tale about Mr. Rockwell back in Missouri, but he is the only man that could have saved me and my daughters from those bloodthirsty bandits. I'm not Mormon, but I believe the Lord uses what he can to bring about good, and you did so much good last week Mr. Rockwell. I'm thankful for you too, Mr. Granstaff, for being here and looking after us."

"Here, here," said Porter, taking a swallow of Valley-Tan and passing the bottle around.

"Well I need some sleep," said Roxy.

"That's a good idea," said Porter. "We're going to need our rest for tomorrow."

"Hope there's no hard feeling about the flatboat, but you understand," said Bill.

Porter just grunted.

Bill held out his hand to finish off the nearly empty bottle of Valley-Tan and Porter reluctantly handed it over.

"I think I'll sit up a spell and watch the fire die," said Quincy.

"Suit yourself," said Porter, as he went to one of the many vacant rooms for some much-needed rest.

Bill and Frenchie stayed too, as the Taggart women also bid their goodnights and retired to the rooms they were using.

Porter was concerned about Quincy staying up with two other men who had been drinking and hadn't been that kind toward his friend. But, Redbone stayed up too, just off in the shadows so Porter decided he would let it play out and get some rest.

As he drifted off to sleep he was pleased to hear some good-natured laughter from the men.

✻✻✻

It was cold, it was rough, yet Shaw still pushed his men hard. Once they were across the Colorado, he gave every man and beast a few moments to dry and get their lungs back.

"We are doing the right thing, never forget. We push ourselves harder than the enemy so that we might triumph at the last, that these heathen murderer's will not get away with their sacrilege. Let's do this." Shaw led them down the rocky shoreline toward the valley.

"He always talk like that?" asked a deputy.

"Yup," answered Matty. "His father was a preacher back in New York. When Joe Smith found that gold bible and started proselytizing, he stole most all of pastor Shaw's flock. You could say he's got some bitterness 'bout that, somewhere."

They rounded the bend in the river, to the valley that stretched out wide. Stars overhead gleamed dully. They hadn't ridden far when they espied the source of the smoke. A white washed stone fort sat at the top of the slope above the river.

"Who is that?"

"Doesn't matter," said Shaw. "They are aiding and abetting a murderer. We ride in hard, guns out and we capture them alive. Do you understand? Only shoot if you have too. I want Porter alive. I am gonna see him hang!"

✳✳✳

Porter was having some surprisingly good dreams when Quincy shook him awake.

"It's time we get a move on. Redbone is pretty antsy."

Porter rubbed his eyes. It was still dark out. "Already? Is it almost dawn?" he asked with a yawn.

"Naw it's probably after midnight, but I talked Bill into selling us the flatboat."

"Really? What'd you offer him?"

"I traded him a bit of that gold I got from the canyon."

"You sure?"

"Yeah, we just gotta hurry. We need to catch that Matamoros bastard."

"All right, all right. I'm up," said Porter. "What about Roxy?"

"She's already up and getting the horses down to the flatboat."

"Good deal. We sure we didn't want to wait for breakfast?"

"Hell's yeah, I'm sure Yankee, let's get going. Don't make too much noise though, we don't want to wake those women folk."

Porter shrugged and followed his friend out the door and into the moonlit courtyard. The embers in the fire pit still glowed, and gave off a whiff of sweet-smelling smoke in the cool evening. Both Frenchie and Negro Bill were passed out near the fire. Two empty bottles of Valley-Tan lying nearby.

"You give them another of my—,"

"Shhhh," Quincy insisted.

"Whay is going on?" asked Porter, as he blinked awake.

They went out the front gate of the fort and took a sloping track down to the river. It glistened in the moonlight like a river of diamonds, while the stars above filled the sky with wondrous twinkling lights.

Roxy already had the horses aboard the flatboat with Redbone's help.

"I'm ready," she said.

"What's that?" asked Porter, at a big lump in the center.

"Oh, it's our supplies and things. Maybe some extra feed for the horses that I found in the barn."

"What barn? Did you buy that from Bill?"

"We traded," she said, rather sheepishly.

"For what?"

"Your Valley-Tan."

"How many?"

"All of them. You need to stay sober on this journey."

"Damnit woman! NO! I want my Valley-Tan!" he shouted, loud enough to wake the dead from the very grip of the grave.

"Quiet!" insisted Quincy. "Help us shove off."

David J. West

"Something ain't right," grumbled Porter. "I need those."

"No, you don't," said Roxy, raising her voice.

"Yes, I do!" he shouted again.

There was some yelling and cursing from up the slope in the fort.

"Great! You woke them up."

"So what? You two stole my hooch."

Quincy said, "We need the flatboat. We gotta hurry, help us push off!"

"I want my whiskey."

"I don't have it. I'm sure its around here somewhere," said Roxy.

"I'm guessing there was no square deal done here. After all I wasn't consulted about my whiskey! Does Bill even know you came up with this trade? He seemed awful unwilling just a few hours ago."

"He'll get over it," said Quincy, putting his whole back into pushing the flatboat off the shoreline. Redbone helped him but the craft still wasn't moving. "Help us, Yankee!"

"I-want-my-whiskey."

"Hold on," said Roxy.

"Where is she going?" questioned Quincy. "Hey! We gotta go now!"

She mounted her horse and kicked its flanks driving it off the flatboat and back toward the fort.

With the sudden decrease in weight, Redbone and Quincy moved the raft a few inches more into the river.

"This would be a whole lot easier with your help," said Quincy.

"I want my whiskey," insisted Porter.

"You're being a child, you know that? A damn child!"

"A child who wants his whiskey!"

The shouting grew louder and Roxy was suddenly riding back from the fort. Bill and Frenchie were on her heels, shouting and cursing.

She rode the horse onto the flatboat and leapt off, hugging two bottles of Valley-Tan. "Here is your damn whiskey, now help us get out of here!"

Port glanced back toward the fort and saw Bill and a half-dressed Frenchie running toward them. "They seem a might upset, but you're right we ought to go." He threw his shoulder into helping push the flatboat, and then it was a few feet out into the river. He leapt aboard as did Quincy and Redbone. Roxy had a pole and was pushing them farther out to catch the current as Bill and Frenchie reached the shoreline.

Frenchie had the longer legs and reached the shoreline first. He strode out into the water til he was hip-deep saying, "C'estnotre bateau." He grasped one end of the flatboat, but was kicked for his troubles by Redbone. He fell back in the cold water gasping and sullenly went back to shore.

"Sorry 'bout that," said Porter.

The flatboat was only a dozen strides out into the river, but it was just far enough that Bill didn't dare go in after it. "That's my flatboat! You stole it! Damn you Mormons!"

"I'm not Mormon," shouted Quincy, with a laugh.

Bill hollered, "Oh, I forgot, you're just a Mormon's Uncle Tom!"

Quincy was almost mad enough to jump in the river to go after Bill, but Roxy held him back.

Porter called out, "Sorry, Bill. I think we were both misled about this trade."

Bill hollered back. "What trade? You son of a bitch?"

"Très peu cool," agreed Frenchie.

"You got my whiskey didn't ya?" shouted Rockwell, as the flatboat drifted farther away.

"No! The woman took the only two bottles I had!" cried Bill.

Porter ignored Bill and frowned at Roxy.

She blushed. "I left him all of it, but when I went back, I only saw these two, so I brought them for you. I don't know what happened to the rest."

The flatboat was now almost to the middle of the river and the current had her cruising at a good speed.

"Bye Bill," shouted Porter. "I'll make it up to you."

"The hell you say!" Bill shouted. Then the river took them around the bend and they were out of earshot.

11. A Dollar Short

Shaw led the charge, the thunder of hooves thumped hard against the sandy ground like war drums. They rounded the front of the fort which faced away from the river. The doors were wide open. Racing inside they had their guns drawn, ready for trouble.

"Where is everybody?" shouted a deputy.

"Look inside, careful like. Remember we want them alive!" shouted Shaw.

Matty dismounted and threw open a door. He carefully held his gun up and ready as he shouted. "Porter? You in there? You best come out peaceful like."

A blonde woman appeared at one of the doors in her nightgown. "What's going on? Who are you?"

"Where is Porter?" barked Shaw, barely keeping his horse under control.

The frightened woman backed away into her dark room.

"You best answer me. I'm territorial Marshal Brody Shaw."

"What do you want with Mr. Rockwell?" the woman asked, a little more defiantly than Shaw would have liked.

"He is a murderer. I'm aiming to bring him to justice. Where is he?"

"I don't know. I thought he was sleeping in the courtyard." She composed herself and said thoughtfully, "But you're wrong about Mr. Rockwell. He is no murderer. He is a hero. He saved me and my girls from that slaver, Matamoros."

Shaw snorted at her answer.

"Ask my girls they will tell you. He singlehandedly killed nine of those desperadoes to save us and a dozen Indian women and children from God knows what fate."

"He ain't no hero," argued Shaw.

Now she became truly defiant, stepping out of her door with her hands on her hips and her words sharp as slander. "Oh really? Let me tell you something Marshal Shaw. Porter came by himself and saved us from the men that killed my husband and violated me and my daughters. Where were you? Where was the U.S. Army? Nowhere to be found. I'll take the heroes you call outlaws any day, and if you don't like it you and yours can just go to hell!"

Shaw was taken aback by her rebuke and let his horse step back a pace from the scorned woman.

"Boss, we got some men out here heading back from down by the river," called Matty from the fort entrance.

"Watch her," said Shaw to one of his deputies then he wheeled his mount about to go out and see to the men, Matty spoke of.

✳✳✳

Bill and Frenchie were trudging back up to the fort, but froze upon seeing the half dozen men on horseback at their very door. "Dog my cats, who the hell is that, now?"

Frenchie didn't have time to answer before the riders barked at them.

"Stay right there! Who are you? Talk fast!"

They weren't shooting yet, so Bill stood his ground. "I'm Bill Granstaff and this is Frenchie. Who are you all?"

A tall rider pushed through his men's horses. "I'm Brody Shaw, territorial Marshal."

"Then I'd like to report a crime."

"Oh?"

"Yes sir, those polecats just now stole my flatboat and are escaping down the river with it."

"Who would that be? I wonder?"

Bill furrowed his brow at Shaw's rude mannerism. "Well, I believe its Orrin Porter Rockwell, a woman calling herself Roxy Lejeune, and a colored man name of Quincy Jackson. They came here on good faith and then stole from me when I said I wouldn't sell them that flatboat."

Shaw gestured at the river. "Matty, Zeke, ride on down and see if you can spot anyone on the water."

Bill and Frenchie started to walk back to the fort but Shaw stopped them with his horse. "Not so fast."

Bill snarled in irritation. "Yes?"

"How do I know you didn't just help Porter escape?"

"Help? He stole my boat! I just told you."

"Like I'm supposed to believe a nigger," Shaw spat.

"Say what?"

"I already heard from the woman up there, and she seems to think awful highly of Rockwell, so why are you changing your story?"

"Changing my story? I just told you everything I know! Porter showed up here this afternoon, made pleasantries and such. Said he was chasing after Matamoros and wanted my flatboat. I got no use for slavers, but I didn't want to sell my flatboat, so his folks got me drinking and then they done took it when I was asleep!"

"Who is the woman then?"

Bill laughed and slapped his knee. "Hell! Just another one of the many problems I seem to have collected from Rockwell. I guess he rescued them a couple weeks back from Matamoros, but then he couldn't take them back to civilization hisself so he told them to come out this way to the fort. Only problem is the Mormons done got run out a little while back by the Utes. So, Frenchie and I took over the place, so now we have to play babysitter to those women folks."

"I'm sorry to be a burden to you, Mr. Granstaff," broke in Mrs. Taggart, "the girls and I will be leaving in the morning. Mr. Shaw, if you really are the law, I would appreciate your escort back to somewhere civilized."

"I didn't mean it like that," said Bill. But Mrs. Taggart just raised a hand to hush him and turned her attention back to Shaw.

Shaw was uncomfortable, he didn't want to have to escort anyone, he was hot on the trail of his prize, the murdering Danite, Porter Rockwell, and now he was being thwarted by petty, little people. Just then, Matty and Zeke came riding up fast.

"They are on the river, Boss!"

Shaw ignored Mrs. Taggart, asking Bill. "Am I right in guessing there isn't anywhere I can catch up to Rockwell?"

"Not without a boat. That's why he needed mine to go after Matamoros."

"Damn it! Hell fires!" Shaw raised his pistol and shot in the air.

The six-gun thundered in the night, the boom echoing off the canyon walls. Most everyone stepped a pace or two back at Shaw's violent outburst.

"Son of a bitch escapes me again!" He cried still waving the six-gun around.

Bill, Frenchie and Mrs. Taggart all backed away a few steps. Even the deputies made a little room for Shaw.

"You know, Boss," offered Matty, "seems these folks got an interesting story to tell and what with all I have heard, I'd imagine it makes for a good case against Rockwell. I say we get it all documented, cuz we know Rockwell is gonna came back sure enough one day and when he does, we just need proof for Judge Spicer."

Shaw looked at Matty and for a half second, Matty wasn't the only one who thought he might get struck down by that piecing gaze. "That is best thing to ever come out of your mouth. We are gonna do just that." He then said to Mrs. Taggart, Bill and Frenchie. "We are gonna be spending the night here. I need every bit of testimony you all have for my case. Mrs. Taggart, I especially need everything you can tell me about what happened to you and your daughters."

She was indignant. "And what about getting us to some relative safety? A town and stage line I'd hope?"

"I'll do that, soon as you help me with my case," said Shaw. He dismounted and led them back toward the fort.

"What do you need from me?" she asked suspiciously.

Bill and Frenchie sulked at the prospect of more unwelcome guests, eating their larder and being a nuisance in general.

Shaw put his arm around Mrs. Taggart. She shivered at his touch. "Now, don't hold anything back. Tell me everything that happened, so I can bring justice to this sad predicament."

"I'll tell you everything I know, but you're not gonna like it," she said.

"Oh? Why not? I just want the truth."

"The truth won't convict Porter Rockwell. My daughter, Emily, will tell you. Emily," she called. There was no answer. Her other daughters appeared. "Where is Emily?"

"How many daughters do you have?"

They shook their heads, and the next eldest, Tana, answered, timidly. "She told me not to worry or say anything, but she is gone. She said she was going to go help Mr. Rockwell."

Mrs. Taggart's face flushed and she turned toward the river. "Emily!" she cried.

"Looks like we better add kidnapping to the charges," said Matty.

A faint smile curled beneath Shaw's mustache.

12. Ride the River

The flatboat glided down the river, free and easy here, and Porter was pleased that in leaving so early they would better close the distance in their pursuit of Matamoros. Every little bit helped in gaining ground. That and, even though it was still dark, he was sure Matamoros wouldn't disembark until much farther downriver, so they were in no danger of missing them at night.

He decided he may as well get a little more sleep, so he took his saddle and bedroll and adjusted a spot near the stack of supplies.

As he punched an area to clear it, it cried out, "Ouch!"

"What the deuce?" Porter tore the canvas off the rations to see Emily Taggart lying there in the stack of hay.

"Hi," she said, sheepishly.

"Hi?" He responded, somewhat surprised at himself with the words. "What are you doing here?"

"Who?" asked Quincy, glancing around then seeing the teenage blonde, he took off his hat and laughed. "Like we needed any more trouble."

"I want to help. I heard you all talking around the fire and thought I'd sure like to help somebody the way you all did me and my sisters, Mr. Rockwell."

Porter grunted, saying, "This ain't the kind of trip you should have stowed away on. This is bad business."

Emily shook her head, the golden curls, stuck with straw, swayed in the moonlight. "I know Matamoros. He is a very bad man and anything I can do to help you I will. I'll do anything, cook, for you, help with the horses, I can shoot. My daddy taught me to shoot before Matamoros killed him."

"Is that why you're here? To get some revenge?" asked Roxy.

"Yes'm. Well, I'd like to see justice done if that's what you mean. I'd like to be there when Mr. Rockwell kills him."

Porter rubbed at his chin. "We're going after a kidnapped girl, hardly any younger than you. This isn't some kind of joyride. This is dangerous. Quint, watch for a spot we can get to shore and drop her off, she ought to be able to walk back to the fort on her own don't ya think?"

"No, I'm not going. I'm here to help you come hell or highwater."

Quincy was holding the steering pole and shook his head. "Funny, she should say that Port, cuz I' can't make that kind of maneuver right now." The river current was moving strong and swift and it was all Quincy could do to keep them in the center of the river, avoiding the many treacherous rocks along the sides.

"Now ya tell me," grumbled Porter, helping Quincy with the steering pole. It operated similar to a rudder albeit much less effectively.

Roxy tried to calm the horses, who nickered and panicked at the sudden rough riding flatboat. Emily got up to help her. Redbone nervously clutched at a rail.

The flatboat went up and down as the river flowed in a rough, white capped barrage. Then, just as suddenly as it had come, it was smooth once again.

"That was awful," said Emily. "I hope there aren't any more stretches like that in store for us."

"I get the feeling we're going to be getting a lot more stretches like that soon enough."

"Likely. No man has ever floated the river through the Grand Canyon below, it's a death trap. We'll find where Matamoros disembarked soon enough."

"Just a couple more hours 'til daylight I think."

"Goodness, that was one of the scariest moments of my life," said Emily.

The others just looked at her, though it seemed Redbone agreed with her.

"How far you suppose we are from the fort now, Quint?"

"I'd bet we're at least twenty miles downriver, maybe more with this current."

Porter rubbed at his beard. "I guess you're with us, Girlie."

Roxy objected, "Porter, no, it's too dangerous for her."

"We're way too far for me to leave her to walk back on her own. We can't give her a horse, and we don't have time to ride her back up there either, not that I think we'd get a very warm reception when we did. She's with us."

"Thank you, Mr. Rockwell."

"Call me Port."

She leaned up and kissed him on the cheek.

Roxy bit her lip and turned around.

Porter sensed this was going to be a longer trip than he had ever anticipated.

13. Debate

"Rise and shine!" hollered Shaw. "We got to get on the trail." The Taggart women were not accustomed to being yelled at. Bill and Frenchie had let them do their own thing in their own time as a courtesy, but this— this was just rude.

"Where are you taking us, Mr. Shaw?"

"It's Deputy Marshal Shaw, Miss Taggart. And I will take you and your girls back to civilization once you show me the remains of the camp you claim Porter liberated you from."

"Why? There isn't anything left there except bodies and a broken down old wagon that we scrounged every last morsel of food from, before we came here."

He gave a wicked grin and poked her in the chest. "Exactly. I want to see that evidence for my own eyes."

She blushed and tried to ignore his impropriety. "What about my daughter? Emily?"

"I don't get the impression that you are too worried about her being with Rockwell."

She didn't answer.

"I think for some strange reason you want to defend him. I don't claim to understand. The man obviously kidnapped your daughter, didn't he?"

"He didn't do that. It doesn't make sense."

"Of course, it doesn't make sense to a peaceful, god-fearing, Christian woman. But let me remind you that Rockwell is a vicious, murderous

Mormon Danite. You have seen him kill. Now, maybe he did save you and your girls' lives, but I assure you that was happenstance."

"No," she countered, with a shake of her head. "He saved us."

Shaw continued, working to change her mind with an intimidating sense of subtlety. "Rockwell had bloodlust on the brain. He had to kill someone, so he waylaid those travelers." He crossed his finger over his neck motion of death, with a grin.

"They were slavers! They murdered my husband, they—"

"Now, now, Miss Taggart, you relax. We will get your daughter back, and we will bring justice to these criminals. I just need you to show me where this happened."

She still argued. "They were killers. He saved us."

Changing tactics, Shaw said, "All right, I believe you. But I need to see it for myself."

"I won't help you in your vendetta against a good man," spat Mrs. Taggart.

"You're fooling yourself," said Shaw. "And that's a sad thing. You really think he is innocent, show me these Mexican slavers. Then I'll exonerate Rockwell and we can worry about other parties."

She went silent, pondering his words.

Bill frowned at the situation, but kept his mouth shut. He was still upset about his flatboat being stolen, but he didn't trust this Shaw a bit either.

"I can show you. You will see that they were bad men who deserved to die. But I need my Emily back. She must have run off thinking she could help Mr. Rockwell."

Matty and the others in the posse, chortled. Shaw glared at his men, demanding silence.

"We will let you show us the way back, and then we will get you ladies to safety in town and we will find your daughter. No matter what. You have my word on it."

Mrs. Taggart felt trapped. She didn't want to do anything to harm Rockwell, he was a savior to her and her girls, but maybe if she could show Shaw the dead slavers, he would know the truth. And this problem could go away for all of them. She prayed Emily was safe.

14. White Water, Red Blood

Sunlight broke high overhead on the red cliffs. The river still moved at a steady pace and the cliffs on both sides seemed to be growing taller by the mile. The flats where they could disembark grew farther and farther between.

"He's got to be landing somewhere soon and when he does, we'll catch him." Rockwell said, as much for himself as the others.

But another twenty miles downriver and there still was no sign of a flatboat or anywhere Matamoros might have camped.

"Could we have missed a spot in the dark where he ran the ferry aground and went on?" asked Quincy.

"I'm worrying at that very thing."

The river widened and slowed, though they were still surrounded by high cliffs on both sides. The occasional sandbar forced them to push off to continue, and they did their best to stick to the center of the river where they could watch both sides and avoid obstacles.

At a particularly wide stretch, the river curved in a great arc, and they found themselves flung to the far left-hand side of the current, as they moved slowly across they stared in surprise.

There on the far right-hand side of the river wedged up on a great sandbar was Matamoros, his seven men, their horses and Kimama!

There was a gasp of shock from both parties. No one had expected this.

Redbone cried out in agony at seeing his daughter with the filthy, dastardly men.

Matamoros laughed and shot at them.

Quincy steered them farther left and let them lodge against the far bank, a few hundred yards downstream of where the robber chief was.

Matamoros and his band took careless pot-shots at them, but stopped once they saw it was fruitless.

Porter and company did not shoot back because Kimama was held forth like a shield.

Redbone raged, but was trapped with nothing more he could do.

"We're in luck, dire as it seems." Porter said.

"How?"

"Even if he gets his flatboat off that bar, he can't go back upstream, the current is too much, and there's no way he can scale those cliffs. He has to come through us. We just got to wait this out."

That didn't sit too well with Redbone, but there was nothing he could do.

They took their own horses off their flatboat to let them graze on the sparse grasses growing there; that and to be sure their mounts didn't become targets. Anything was better than being stuck on the flatboat all day. Emily made herself busy, frying up some of their rations, which Porter noticed were considerably more than they had when they had left Price.

"Did you help yourself to a few things of Bill's?"

"I did. He said we could help ourselves to his stores whenever we left, so I did."

"I'm sure he meant you and your mama, all of you going back to somewhere civilized."

"I know but I wanted to contribute. Oh, and I brought your Valley-Tan whiskey. I knew it meant a lot to you, so, when Roxy wasn't looking, I brought four bottles down to the flatboat. You have it all except for those two you drank last night," she said, with a bright smile.

"I didn't drink two. Everybody else did." It was hard to be mad at a girl that smiled so much, especially when she had brought him more of his prized possessions. "But thank you anyhow."

"How long are we going to have to wait here?"

"Until we get Redbone's daughter back I suppose. I wouldn't be too worried though, we've got him in a good spot, he can't get past us, and I'm sure we probably have more rations than he does. We can wait him out."

"What can we do though if he has the girl?"

"I expect he'll parley with us soon. I'll tell him we're willing to let him go if he'll let the girl go.

"Do you think he will?'

"No. Men like him only understand one thing and that's usually a bullet."

"That why god made men like you?"

"I suppose so."

Redbone never took his eyes off Matamoros, while the others saw to their own chores and prepared.

A half hour later and several more attempts at shooting Porter and the others, Matamoros finally called out, "Why do you want me so bad, huh Marshal? I am only trying to leave your god-forsaken country, eh? Why not just let me leave in peace, and you will be left in peace too, huh? I swear I will never come back to your country."

"Simple. Let the Ute girl go!"

A wild shot near them was the first response.

Matamoros shouted over the roar of the river. "I don't know if I can do that. You see, what would I have to give me assurance of a safe passage back to my home country, huh? You see the predicament I'm in don't you, Gringo?"

"We ain't ever gonna stop dogging your trail til we get her back."

"What is so special about this one huh? You already freed all the Goshutes I had and those white women too, huh? You cost me a lot of dinero! A lot of men, you killed so many, I weep for them."

"Good."

"That was unkind Gringo, you killed so many of mi amigo's. What will I tell their families, huh?"

"I didn't think those bastards had families," yelled Port.

Quincy joined in, "Think of all the money we saved you in having to pay them."

"You are so mean, Gringo, so mean. But, I think I will keep this one, huh? To keep me warm at night and then maybe I slit her throat when I am done. You want that to happen? You let me go, no molestado, huh?"

"I'm gonna give you the peace of a bullet," Porter shouted.

"I guess we have an argument then, huh? Fine, but you will be sorry. You see the two amigo's waiting for me with the flat boat, were only some of my men on this journada del muerto. I have more. You will see them soon, and then what? You will have come all this way just to die? So sad, so pointless. We will get past you now, and you had better let us go with no molestado."

Matamoros held Kimama in front of him as the five Apache and two Mexican's finished pushing the flatboat off the sandbar. "You see? We are ready to continue our journada. Are you willing to let her die?"

"You ain't taking her to Mexico," shouted Porter.

"We shall see."

They pushed the flatboat free into the river and it slid toward Porter's position. Matamoros still held Kimama in front of him to dissuade their shooting at him. But, he had discounted the accuracy at which Porter and Quincy could fire.

They each fired, and an Apache went down on the far right, while Quincy took a Mexican on the far left. They reengaged, but now the men scrambled for cover behind their horses, even Matamoros, who still held the girl close.

"We gonna shoot their horses?" asked Quincy.

That made Porter terrible mad, he sure didn't want to kill an innocent animal, but he wasn't about to let Matamoros just slip away.

"Yeah, shoot 'em."

They fired, Roxy and Redbone too. The horses on the flatboat screamed and several tumbled from the raft. The chaos aboard had the Apache returning fire while dodging their own maddened beasts.

Then Porter saw something he sure didn't expect. A small canoe-like skin boat released from the side of the flat-boat with Matamoros and Kimama aboard. It slipped into the water out ahead of the flatboat. The girl looked unconscious and Matamoros sped ahead of the flatboat with the remaining men throwing as much lead Porter's way as possible.

They had lost several horses, but it seemed like they didn't care. Perhaps Matamoros wasn't lying and he had more men waiting for him farther downstream. If so he would have more horses in any case.

A cloud of smoke belched from the mass of Apache shooting.

The skin-boat zipped past their position and Redbone cried out in anguish. He rushed toward the shore to see his daughter, but the hail of bullets sent him ducking back down for cover.

Without a hostage to worry about, Porter and company let loose a great volley of lead.

The shooting thundered in the canyon, drowning out the subtle roar of the river. Emily held her hands over her ears, hidden behind cover. She might have been screaming at the noise, Porter wasn't sure, he couldn't hear anything either.

The flatboat drifted down river enveloped in the cloud of smoke.

"What do we do?" asked Roxy.

"Same as always, we keep after them. Matamoros can go faster in that skin boat, but we'll catch him. Get our horses back on board, get gotta get moving and stay close so they can't surprise us around another bend."

It only took a few moments to get the horses loaded and they were heading downriver with only about a quarter mile between them and the next boat. The few remaining Apache still fired occasionally, just to gauge the distance but it was too great to be a threat.

"Were all their horse's dead?" asked Quincy.

82

Porter nodded grimly. "Think so, unless they had one or two trained good enough to lie down on a boat, that'd be tough even for horsemen as skilled as the Apache."

Quincy hung his head. "I sure didn't like doing that. We did it a few years back in a battle with the Comanche. We had no cover somewhere down toward Yucca Flats and it was all we could to save our own skins. I swore, I'd never shoot another horse."

Porter just clapped Quincy on the shoulder. He didn't like doing it either, but the life of a girl mattered more than any animal.

The canyon narrowed a spell and, in turn, the river grew faster and had a few more white caps complimented with jutting boulders. On top of that, they got closer to the other flatboat and the shooting commenced in earnest.

"Quint! You man the steering pole. Roxy, Emily, Redbone, do what you can for the horses, I'll keep their heads pinned down," shouted Porter. He took out his Winchester rifle and began sending rounds downrange at the Apache.

His foes had the benefit of dead horses for cover, but Porter knew once he got close enough, the heavy caliber was capable of punching through the dead meat and touching the men on the other side. In fact, he was counting on it.

Lead flew in both direction and one of the horses behind Porter screamed as it took a bullet in the neck. It flailed and kicked then dropped overboard as a particularly nasty bump in the river sent them all careening to one side and then the other.

With a startled cry, Emily fell overboard.

David J. West

Roxy whipped around and tossed a rope to the shocked girl who snatched it just before it was pulled from beyond her reach.

"I can't see where I'm going!" shouted Quincy, doing his best to keep the flatboat in the center of the river. Redbone helped pull Emily back aboard. "Staying in the water might have been the safest spot," said Quincy.

Emily was only too relieved to clamber back aboard. "I don't know how to swim," she chattered.

"You might have been safer in the water," Quincy shouted.

Another horse plunged into the rapids. Porter stole a glance to see which one when a bullet nipped at his hat. He turned and rapid fired his full chamber right back.

Redbone moved beside Porter, firing his own long gun. He cried aloud in triumph at hitting a man dead center and seeing him fall into the churning, white water.

No one was controlling the Apache flatboat and it hit the boulders with reckless abandon, tipping the craft almost a third of the way up, granting the men aboard no cover at all. But they didn't dare try to stand and control it either.

A boulder caught the flatboat, holding it tipped and stationary for a moment and now Roxy too was shooting dead center of mass.

One of the Apache leapt away into the white water, while the last two-remaining kept firing their rifles. Somewhere in the combined lead tornado, Porter got them all. Then just as suddenly, the flatboat released and continued downriver, bobbing to and fro, empty of life.

"Was that all of them?"

"Except for the one that leapt overboard, but he ain't gonna be in no position to shoot at us. I don't think he even had his rifle when he jumped."

"Porter, we lost three horses."

He turned and sure enough, two had leapt away and were gone, one lay on its side bleeding out and the other two looked skittish as hell.

"Damnit!"

It was Porter's stallion that was bleeding out. He dropped to his knees and put a hand on the bullet wound. He caressed the animals neck and glanced at his friends, worried. "He was a good one. One of the best I've ever ridden." He put his Navy Colt up to the animal's head.

"No!" screamed Emily. "Let me see what I can do."

"What? He's lost too much blood.

"Please let me try."

"I don't want him to be in pain, Girl."

"Please let me." Her tears fell freely.

"All right, but if you can't do anything, I don't want him suffering."

"Thank you," said Emily. She tore open a knapsack from the ration bundle and worked feverishly at cleaning the wound. "Papa, used to work on horses, I learned a lot from him," she said.

Porter grimaced. He sure wanted her to be right, hoping that there was some kind of miracle she could work, but he had his doubts. He'd seen too many horses take minor wounds and drop dead a few miles down the trail. It was hard business; a man gets close to a good horse, especially one so talented and true as the stallion. Porter had leapt the canyon back in the San Rafael Swell with him, which was something no one had ever done. He was a good horse. Porter then realized he had never actually named the animal, he just thought of it as The Stallion.

Roxy clutched Porter's hand, then realized he still had blood all over it. She squeezed, and wiped her hand off on the pine guardrail. "I'll say a prayer. Good horses are hard to come by, especially one you get the day you should have died."

Porter nodded. "I can't ever forget that," he said soberly. He grabbed one of his bottles of Valley-Tan and took a good hard swallow.

Quincy smacked Porter's shoulder for the bottle. Port handed it to him.

"May I?" asked Emily, still on her knees beside the horse.

Port's eyebrows raised in surprise. But he decided she was old enough to choose for herself, and he handed her the bottle. Emily didn't take a drink, but instead poured some on the wound, then fished out a slug with a long pair of tweezers.

"I'll be damned," said Porter in surprise.

"Probably," Roxy scolded.

"I think, he'll be all right," said Emily, as she stitched the wound closed.

"You are an angel, sent from Heaven above," said Porter.

Emily blushed.

Roxy frowned.

Quincy laughed as he was steering the flatboat around another bend in the river. Then his eyes perked up. "Porter! Right over there." He pointed at the far-left bank.

The Apache who jumped overboard was just climbing out of the water. He stared at them with dark, angry eyes.

"What do you want to do?"

"Dunno. He is disarmed. I won't shoot him. He'll probably be trapped and die in this canyon."

A shot rang out. Emily and Roxy both gasped at the sudden shock of it. The Apache wavered and fell back into the river.

Redbone stood there with his rifle still smoking. "No man may take my family from me."

The dead Apache floated downriver beside them, his bright, red blood mingling with the red-brown river until they couldn't see the vibrant discoloration anymore.

"Fair enough," grunted Porter.

15. Hounds on the Scent

Matamoros had the lead again, as his skin boat could maneuver faster down the river than they could in the flatboat, but once they landed, they had a couple horses and he didn't. Porter prayed it was a worthwhile tradeoff.

Redbone hung off the front rail of the flatboat watching hawk-like for any sign of Matamoros on the shoreline on both sides as they went downriver.

"Will we even be able to catch him?" asked Roxy.

Porter grunted in the affirmative. "We will, we just have to keep our eyes peeled on the banks, like Redbone there. It's the only way we can be sure. If I was Matamoros, I'd get off the river soon as I could and hope we kept going by. One benefit of these canyon walls is he has nowhere to go just yet, but once it opens up and there are beaches and spots between the cliffs we need to be concerned, then we gotta be real vigilant."

"Where could a man even run to in a land like this but death?" asked Roxy, as she stared up at the high cliff walls.

"I'm sure he'll take the eastern trail and hook back up with the Old Spanish Trail again."

"I thought we got off that back at the mission."

"We did and we didn't. There are a few different forks, but they all converge eventually."

The river twisted and turned this way and that until it was a maddening back and forth current driving Roxy to tears. The high canyon walls shielded them from the sun and, in so doing, it never allowed the spray of the river soaking their clothing to fully dry before another rogue wave hit them and it started all over again. It was chilly.

By mid-day some of the canyon walls dropped just a little. Here and there the sloping canyon walls gave way to a few beaches of solid stone and sandy mud. These were precarious places a person could conceivably land. They all watched, eager to find where Matamoros might make his landfall.

Off to their left, a new river fed into the Colorado, and there were some peculiar tracks along the stony shore nearby.

"Let's head over to that finger of rock and take a look, but let's be careful, he might snipe at us."

"I don't see anywhere a person could hide," said Emily, motioning at the bare-faced, red-orange canyon walls. "This is all plain as day to me. I wouldn't know where to hide here."

"That's what worries me," grumbled Porter, as he steered the flatboat across the entwining currents. Redbone and Quincy helped with poles, pushing along the bottom to better guide them swiftly to the shore.

As they came closer they saw a skin boat had landed, but there were a lot of hoof prints there to greet Matamoros.

"His men?"

"I'd imagine so, don't know who else he would dare draw up to," drawled Porter. He was silently counting the hoof prints.

"How many?" asked Quincy.

"At least five, maybe six. It's six, not counting Matamoros. There were ten horses, but I only see six men's boot leathers milling about here and here."

Redbone knelt and ran his hand over a print that was clearly his daughter's moccasin pressed into the fragile dried mud. "Two hours," he said, grinding his teeth.

"Guess we should be glad they didn't wait around to ambush us, huh?" asked Quincy.

"Yup," agreed Porter.

"How do we catch them?"

"We—can't. Not with only three horses between the five of us."

"What are you saying?" asked Roxy. She put her hands on her hips and gave the sternest look she could muster.

"I'm wondering if maybe Redbone and I ought to go after them, and you three make your way back to the Mission slow and easy with my horse."

"No," insisted Roxy. "We're here to help and you need all of that you can get."

"I'm with Roxy, we need to stick together," said Quincy.

Emily vehemently shook her head in over exaggerated agreement.

Redbone scowled, saying, "We must hurry, Blood Brother."

Porter cursed, "Hell-fires! I can't please everyone!"

"It's not safe, to run off with just Redbone, he's too hot-headed right now. We gotta work on this together," insisted Quincy. "Besides you're gonna need more guns on your side."

Porter snarled and wiped his face in frustration. "Redbone, I know you don't like it but we gotta stick together for support. We're gonna travel slow and easy. Two to a horse except mine since he's wounded. Good thing the women folk ain't too heavy."

Both Roxy and Emily stared daggers at Porter.

"What?" asked Porter, with his hands outstretched. "I didn't say you were fat."

"You shouldn't have said anything," scolded Roxy.

"I can't win with you," muttered Porter.

"The hell you say," joked Quincy.

Redbone did not dismount. He beat his chest twice, saying, "No. I go on alone."

"No, you won't!" cried Roxy. As she went to stand in front of his horse.

Redbone stared hard at her and urged his horse to go around her.

"You need our help and we need yours. We stick together," cried Porter, just as the war-chief started to trot away. "Don't make me regret helping you! You hear me!"

Redbone was trotting away but wheeled his horse around. "I cannot let them destroy her."

"Matamoros won't. If he was going to do that, he would have already. We will catch them, but we can't go running into a trap, or running horses to death either."

Redbone brought his mount back to them and leapt down from the fine Spanish saddle, snarling. "I need drink."

Porter nodded and pulled a bottle of Valley-Tan from his saddle bags and handed it to Redbone; who popped the cap and took a long deep guzzle and then another and another.

"Is that a good idea?" asked Roxy.

"Man's gotta deal with everything his own way. He'll be all right."

Roxy pursed her lips in a disbelieving scowl. "We should get moving."

Porter nodded. "Emily, ride with Redbone. You two," he said, swinging a gnarled finger and pointing at Roxy and Quincy on the bay horse.

"Yes, your majesty," said Roxy, giving a false curtsy in her dirty black and red dress.

Emily blinked in shock at that display. She was only a year or two younger than Roxy, but was unaccustomed to seeing such behavior. "If I would have ever said that to my Pa, he would have licked me good."

Roxy shrugged.

"With a belt!" Emily emphasized. "You ought to be nicer to him."

Roxy narrowed her gaze at Emily until her nose scrunched, then just shook her head in disgust and sighed, "You have no idea who my father is do you?"

"Mr. Lejeune?"

"Ha! How about the most powerful man in the west?"

Emily looked at Porter and Quincy. "Is she crazy?"

"Maybe a little bit." Porter grinned, but then turned to care for his stallion's wounds. Emily's work had stopped the bleeding, but Porter worried the stallion might never be able to jump like it had. He would have to take it very careful riding the animal for some time. He adjusted the saddle, reins and stirrups and gingerly climbed into the saddle. "Let's get as far as we can before dark."

They mounted up and followed the very definite trail of the fleeing kidnappers as it rose and climbed the hills above the river.

16. Land of the Dead

They were lucky, no, blessed that there had been a few recent rains this season, otherwise they would have been bust. Scanty pools, little more than mudholes, dotted the desert and gave sustenance enough for them to keep going. Several times they were forced to dig and gain what moisture they could for themselves and their animals. It was not a healthy pursuit but they were undeterred.

Porter knew they were slowly, but surely, falling farther and farther behind. They simply could not ride as hard as the bandits, but as long as they persisted, they still had the path ahead of them.

The trail here was testament to the harshness of the desert; every day they saw its victims by the wayside. Some forms that used to be men were now dried out husks, resembling mummies with their teeth jutting out in hollow cries that caught the wind and silently screamed. The bleached bones of horses and oxen were here too, picked clean by scavengers.

The nights were cold up on the high desert and they typically had no fire to light because there was no fuel to be had. This was a dead land peopled only with ghosts and haunted memories. The grey moonbeams lit the rolling landscape, making it seem as if everything was bathed in dark ice. Morning was always welcomed despite their sore bones and dire need to press on.

After four days, it got worse.

A storm rolled in, it was full of wind, wrath, and thunder without the rain. The gusts blasted them and stole anything that wasn't securely tied down.

"We need shelter!" cried Quincy, his voice hardly heard above the gale.

Emily's light blue shawl was scooped up, brandished twenty feet in the air before them, and then whisked far away to the east.

Porter held his hat securely to his head and glanced about in what should have been a bright afternoon day. Dust blinded them and they could see only a dozen paces in any direction.

"My gut says let's see what the horses feel guided too!" He hollered back.

It was agreed upon and the five of them struggled together, holding tight to their reins and hats, and trudged blindly alongside their animals.

They soon found a thicket with a few boulders nearby that seemed to give a mocking semblance of shelter, at least from one side or another. It was a miserable, restless afternoon with a weak sun and biting sand in the face. By evening, the winds vanished as suddenly as they had come, but the billowing dust had erased any sign of the trail they had followed. There was no trail anymore.

17. Double Cross

Shaw led the posse and Taggart women over the wide plains, through the red hills, and back over the desolate wastes. They found the wagon of the slavers, though others had stripped near everything of value from it. The buckboard and tailgate were both gone. There was almost no remnant left of the cotton top and even a wheel had been taken. The broken one left behind by whomever had scavenged this vehicular corpse.

It was plain enough there had been several bodies here. The flies still buzzed in wanton abandon, but the carcasses had been dragged off by coyotes and other predators.

"See, this is what I told you. This was our wagon. My husband was killed by those slavers and left to rot out in the open air somewhere to the west."

Shaw dismounted and examined what little he could. "How many bodies you count, Matty?"

"At least six, no, over there is a seventh."

Shaw agreed and traipsed around until he found an eighth in the wagon itself, the source of most of the flies. A ninth was dragged farther than the others and curled up beneath a big sage.

"Reckon he wasn't quite dead, but sure wished he was. Must have crawled under that bush to get away from the sun after everyone else had left. Choking of thirst is mighty cruel."

"Bad way to go," lamented Matty.

"Choking is the worst," agreed another posse member.

Mrs. Taggart and the girls were displeased with their escorts assessment.

"These men had it coming. They are all having dinner with the devil himself," snarled Mrs. Taggart. "Can't you tell? My girls and I told you the truth. These were the scum of the earth. Slavers from Mexico. They violated us and countless others. I hope they rot in hell for all eternity."

Shaw gave a half-smile and nodded, but answered, "Maybe."

"Maybe?" Mrs. Taggart repeated in shock.

"It's hard to tell anything with the way things have been left here. Matty, see if you can't dig out a few of the rounds stuck in that wagon. I want to be able to say they are Rockwell's .45's."

"What do you mean maybe?"

"I gotta get to the truth of the matter. Like you said, you women have been through a lot. Maybe you can't remember the truth. Being in this place can be a delirious encounter. Maybe none of you are in your right minds any longer."

"Oh, yes I can. I remember the truth."

"I don't think so. I think Rockwell murdered your husband and these others so he could steal your daughter when he thought it most convenient. I've seen it before."

Mae Taggart's mouth dropped in shock, but she quickly composed herself, shouting, "You dirty liar! You're looking for evidence of a crime that never occurred. You're a two-timing polecat!"

"Matty, shut her up with a gag if she can't be civil. We're heading back to Ferry-Town, and we are gonna wait just a little while until I figure out where we are gonna lay in wait. Let's get a move on."

18. The Uninvited

Their camp was situated with the wide open plain stretched out before them and tall red buttes behind. A small smattering of dried out juniper scrub brush gave them enough fuel for a decent fire. With the campfire blazing in front of them it felt like they finally had a sheltered space though it certainly wasn't any safer than any other flat place they had found. This was just cozier.

The stars were bright and the moon was cold, and somewhere a coyote howled a lonesome cry.

"Are we still on the right trail?" asked Roxy. Her tone was hopeful despite her slouching near the fire for warmth.

"Yeah, I'm sure. There's no way he would go farther southwest into the desert, he is heading east, back to the Old Spanish Trail. With any luck, they hit the same storm we did and will be just as paralyzed. We can hope they got it worse than we did and they lost all their horses."

"Now that would be something sweet," said Quincy.

Redbone stood at the edge where shadow and firelight met and wrestled. He was wrestling on the inside too, to keep his stony visage intact when all of them knew he was as broken-hearted as any man could be.

"We're gonna get her back, Redbone. I swear it," said Quincy.

Redbone murmured at him in acknowledgment, but then turned away again.

Quincy looked to Porter who just shrugged in response.

"I'm just being encouraging," he said.

"I hear you, but the Indian don't always think like we do. They have their own way of thinking about time and distance. I bet this has been the longest week of his life."

"Something approaches," said Redbone. "On foot."

That was as surprising to him as any of them. Nobody just walked out in the desert unless their horse was dead and they were almost dead themselves. Everyone, except Emily, knew that fate incredibly well.

The horses were the next to notice. Their eyes flared and they stamped in a panic, as if a catamount were about to drop upon them. They pulled on their reins that had them fixed to a great dry stump of juniper. The bindings held, but the thing heaved at their pressure.

"Is it a man?" asked Porter.

Redbone didn't take his eyes off the advancing man. "It walks like one."

It almost looked like an Indian, but certainly not of any recognizable tribe. He had sun-darkened, red skin and wore a faded Navajo blanket over his shoulders. The buckskins were too tight and they were torn and dirty, ripped apart at the seams as if they might have belonged to a child's corpse and were stolen. Wisps of long, thin hairs teased at his chin and jowls, just faint enough to be visible yet not grant what anyone would call a true beard. His hair was black, but with occasional streaks of grey peppered throughout. It was dirty, long and unkempt and there was something odd about his eyes. They weren't right, almost like they were too dark and had no visible whites. But the worst thing was the smell, a horrid stench preceded him like a cloud. It was like a wet dog, if that dog was also dead and left to rot in the sun for a week.

But he spoke pretty fair English. "Greetings to the camp. May I come in?"

One of the horses screamed in fright.

Porter scrutinized him, looking at him this way and that. Redbone who stood not five paces from the stranger appeared frozen. "No," Porter answered, his hand on the pommel of his six-gun. "You're not invited."

"Porter!" insisted Roxy.

Port stole a glance away from the dirty man to flash his eyes with a grim intensity at Roxy, silently telling her to be still. Quincy had one hand on his gun and the other on his belly.

Emily was petrified and kept peeking over her shoulder behind them, until she wrapped herself up in her blanket and ignored the dirty stranger.

"Are you sure? I could be of some benefit to you and yours."

"No. Go away," insisted Porter. His trigger finger itched something terrible fierce while his left hand was on his blessed Bowie knife's hilt. "Leave. Now."

"But it is so cold. Let me warm myself at your fire for but a moment, and then I shall travel on."

"No," Porter stated flatly.

The dirty man smirked and took a few steps to the left, as if he would not come any closer but was circling about an invisible wall. "Woman. Take pity on me and let me warm myself by your fire. I am so hungry. I am so cold."

Roxy looked at Porter. Emily peeked out from her blankets then hid beneath them again. Redbone was still frozen in place.

Quincy dripped sweat, thinking he needed to act, to shoot to do something, but instead vomit came erupting out like a dam burst in his guts.

"Quincy!" cried Roxy, rushing to Quincy's side.

"I'm all right," he said, coughing as he spat the last of it out of his mouth. His blinked, looking at the stranger. Tears streamed from his eyes.

Porter steeled himself to calm things down for the sake of the others. "You can't come into our camp. You are not invited. Leave."

The dirty man appeared like he would venture closer, but never took that final step into the invisible perimeter of their camp. It was an almost imperceptible balance of where the firelight and shadow met, arcing a circle around them.

"Porter, at least let him have some fire," said Roxy.

"That ain't what he wants," growled Porter.

Roxy was about to say something, but Porter cut her off. "Fine, watch." He pulled a long branch from the flames. It was burning on one end, all orange and crisp black. He tossed it at the feet of the dirty man. "There you go, some fire, some warmth. Go away and make your own camp."

The dirty man gestured toward Emily and said, "My child, come with me and leave these others behind."

Despite her fear, she sat up as if she might consider his invitation.

But Porter put a hand on her shoulder and forced her back down on her rump.

The dirty man beckoned to her one more time and this time Porter had to be more forceful in making her sit back down. Redbone still stood petrified and unseeing.

Roxy looked from the dirty man to Porter to Emily and back to Quincy. "What's going on?" she asked.

"The thing is leaving. One way or t'other." growled Porter, as he drew his pistol and leveled it at the dirty man thing. "Leave!"

"Porter, no! He's unarmed."

"Come," said the Uninvited.

"You don't think I should shoot a wolf at the door, coming for your child? That's what this thing is."

The dirty man ignored the burning torch, smirked again, and walked away into the darkness leaving the light to flicker against the cold ground and diminish. Once they could no longer see him, the horses calmed and relaxed, leaving off their stretched tethers.

Redbone became himself once again, blinking and giving a questioning look to Porter on how a burning torch could have found itself at the edge of their camp. It was as if he had not witnessed anything that had just transpired.

"What the hell was that?" asked Quincy. "That man's stink made my stomach churn. And his eyes, Lord, and here I thought you had a creepy stare."

"I don't think it was man, but I couldn't say what it was exactly. There's things out here, haunts, ghouls, skin-walkers and such. But they can't come into your home or space unless they're invited. I can't explain it; maybe the angels watching over you or something keep them at bay. Those things are walking death, but they have limitations. And we just witnessed it."

"I don't know that I'm gonna be able to sleep," said Quincy.

"What was here?" asked Redbone, glancing about at the gloom.

Porter looked at Roxy and Quincy, saying, "See, and I swear Redbone doesn't even have a sense of humor."

Redbone's brow furrowed in confusion. "Blood Brother. What was here?"

"One of them Haunts. It's gone, I told it that it wasn't invited."

Quincy took a drink from his canteen. "This ain't enough. I need coffee."

Redbone gasped in relief. "I was afraid I was losing my mind. I thought someone was coming and then, I remember nothing."

"That is what they do."

Quincy spat and fixed himself another cup of coffee. "I ain't sleeping tonight. Oh, Hell, no!"

19. Ruin

Passing through the desert, they were lucky to find a few pools of rainwater for the horses. They took turns being stingy with the canteens themselves. While the tracks of Matamoros's men had vanished, Porter was sure he had found the Old Spanish Trail. Still, they knew were getting farther behind with each passing day.

When they took a break that evening, Roxy came up to Porter and asked, "Why did that Haunt try to get Emily to go with him?"

"I don't know, but I'm sure it wasn't for anything good."

"But what do you think?"

Porter shrugged but said, "Maybe he wanted to eat her."

"That's awful. You really think so?"

"I don't rightly know. But there are some powerful evil things in this world."

She looked out at the red sunset. "Do you think we'll see that thing again?"

"I hope not, but this is a strange land. Anything is possible." With that, he pulled his hat down over his face and said in a muffled tone. "Tell Quint, he has first watch. I'm spent."

Roxy took her time going back to the others, who were still caring for the horses and setting up a campfire with the meager scraps of wood they had cobbled together. All day long any branch of scrub was picked up for the sake of having something for the night. It still didn't amount to much. This was a dead land.

"You've got first watch, Quincy," she called.

Roxy ran her fingers through her hair and watched the sun set. She couldn't see anything moving on the horizon, but had a bad feeling that they hadn't seen the last of that uninvited thing. It made her skin crawl and she absently ran her hand along the pommel of her six-gun. It gave small comfort.

"You've got first watch, Quincy. Porter said," she said.

"Porter said? Porter said," grumbled Quincy.

"I did," shouted Porter, from beneath his hat.

"Fine."

***

Emily woke up screaming. She dreamed the uninvited man was ensnaring her in a web of shadows. Drums throbbed in her head, but when she awoke, there was no other sound but her companions asking what was wrong. No drums, no web of shadows, no uninvited dirty man.

"I'm all right. It was just a nightmare. It seemed so real though, I was sure for a moment there I was captured by that terrible man."

"By who? Matamoros again?"

"No. The dirty shadow man. The one we saw last night. Do you think he is following us? Why did I dream about him?"

Roxy held her hand to soothe her.

Porter rubbed at his beard while adjusting his hat. "Dunno. Maybe his kind can invade dreams and such. Redbone?"

The war-chief gritted his teeth before answering. "It is not good to talk about such things. It can invite them."

Roxy prodded, "Is there anything we can do to help him stay away and out of her head?"

Redbone nodded. He took some sage from a leather satchel and placed it to smolder on the dying coals a moment. Then he stood and walked around their camp in a circle, chanting softly as he waved the smoking incense about.

It was near on morning and no one was about to sleep, so they got back on the trail and wandered through the vast, lonely desert. Sometimes a buzzard high overhead broke up the strange stillness, but most of the time there was literally nothing to see besides the blue sky and red brown rolling hills. Nary a bush or plant of any kind grew here, and it became wearisome just being within such a scene.

They camped for the night in a wide plain, and, at the least, there were no more nightmares for anyone that night. The next day was more of the same and the same after that. But on the fourth day through the dreary desert, they smelled water.

Coming up over a rise, they looked and saw a brilliant sun-flecked river twisting beneath them like a serpent.

"I think I know where they are holed up," said Porter.

20. The Fort

There was a wide stretch of river before them and beyond that was an old Spanish fort. It was 'L' shaped and its walls, while not terribly high, certainly looked thick. Jagged stone was carefully set and the small apertures for shooting were deep and evenly spaced along the perimeter. Logs made the rafters and smaller trees were woven over the top and covered in sod for the roof. A man on horseback could probably leap to the roof but then what?

"If they are in there, it's suicide to go near it," said Quincy. "At least if we were to try during the day. Maybe tonight?"

Redbone gave his agreement by the swift swinging of his hatchet.

Porter rubbed at his beard. "I'm not sure anyone is in there. No smoke, so sound, no sign of life just yet."

"Maybe it's a trick? Get us to just ride up to be in range of the guns?"

"That's always possible too."

Redbone challenged. "Perhaps it is the same as the one with the other black man and the French. Perhaps friends are inside there too." It was plain that he wanted to rush down and find out.

"You think Matamoros would be stopping anywhere that might have a friend of ours?" asked Porter, shaking his head.

Redbone turned away, obviously feeling foolish for the suggestion.

"So, what do we do?" he asked.

Quincy sided with Redbone this time. "We're burning daylight with every minute we wait somewhere."

"True, but the horses need a good rest and rubdown. We wait and see if there is any sign of occupation. Either way, we move careful."

"Why wait?" asked Emily. "That place might be warmer."

"It ain't safe. We don't know what's down there," said Roxy.

"We wait til we know a little more," agreed Porter.

Redbone didn't like that answer. "Enough talk. If my daughter is there, I will find out!" He leapt atop his horse and kicked its flanks to ride down the hillside and across the river. White water splashed at his mounts hooves.

The rest of them expected to hear the crack of a rifle, but there was nothing. His horse swam the swift river and then clambered up the steep bank. Redbone was only a hundred yards from the fortress. He turned to look bac at the others and signaled them to follow.

"What do we do?" asked Quincy.

Porter shrugged but he drew his rifle from his scabbard. Then took careful aim across the river at the fort. If somebody started shooting at Redbone, he'd return lead in kind. "We're running low on ammunition, so I am reminding everyone to be conservative."

Redbone was only twenty feet from the forts walls when shots rang out and his horse was struck in the neck. He reared screaming and tumbled over. The quick war-chief rolled away and scrambled back to the river's edge where the snipers could not reach him. A cacophony of lead filled the air before suddenly going still. Echoes died in the distance like ghosts retreating.

Porter stared down his barrel but couldn't make out a target.

"You gonna do anything or just stare?" asked Quincy.

"I've got no target. I couldn't even tell which of those peep holes the shots came from. Redbone will be all right, he's got cover so long as they don't come charging out, he'll be able to snake back to us soon enough. Trouble is we're down another horse now."

Roxy rocked back and forth on her heels; her gun wandering between her palms. "And if they come charging out at him?"

"I'll shoot 'em. But I don't think they will. They'll hole up in there and use a fort for what it's made for, holding off enemy attacks. They might think there is a whole tribe out there besides just us."

"Doesn't Matamoros know it's just us?"

"We don't even know he is in there. He might have just passed through and we have a Spanish garrison. Either way, they've got more guns than we do. We gotta be smart."

No one came out of the fort. Gradually dusk crept over the horizon and with the cover of night, Redbone slid back across the river to the camp.

21. Double Back

"Did you see what a damn fool thing that was to do?" griped Porter.

"He knows," said Roxy, putting her hand on Redbone's shoulder. He sat with his head down. "Beating him over the head about it won't help."

"Now we're down a horse. We can't afford that."

"He knows!" argued Roxy, the tone in her voice downright nasty to Porter's ears.

"I will get many more horses and then my Blood Brother will forgive me," he said under his breath.

"Hell, I forgive you, ya impatient cuss. We just better hope we can get these horses soon."

"Everyone makes mistakes, Porter," grumbled Roxy.

"I said I forgave him. Let it go, Little Sister."

She sniffed and gently patted Redbone on the back as if to say that she was there to defend him. He looked over his shoulder at her a little puzzled.

Porter rubbed at his beard, like he always did when he was thinking. "Well, say we ride on past the fort and see if we can't find some tracks. To determine if Matamoros is already gone or if he is holed up in there. If he's gone, there's no need for us to do anything about the fort. We just keep trailing after Matamoros slow as we are."

"And if he is still there?" asked Roxy.

"Then we better come up with a damn good way of yanking him out. It won't be easy. Those things are made to withstand serious Indian attacks. They'll have plenty of food and a well for sure."

"And horses," said Redbone.

"That's right, and horses."

"So—" began Roxy.

"Redbone and I will go and check it out. You three stay put and out of sight. We don't want them seeing a campfire and coming to get you. Not that I think they would."

"That's comforting," said Emily, breaking her vow of silence for the evening.

"You wanted to come along, girl. This is dangerous business."

"We'll be fine," said Quincy.

"Good man, Quint. I expect we'll be a few hours," said Porter, as he mounted his horse. Then he and Redbone disappeared into the night, silent as phantoms.

"You sure we're all right?" asked Emily.

"If you was in a fort, well-guarded and stocked with food, would you come out into the dark to fight some Indians hiding out in the brush across the river?"

"No," said Emily, shaking her head vehemently.

"Exactly. I say we go over that hill and get us a campfire going, just for a little warmth and some hot coffee."

Roxy reluctantly agreed, finding no fault in Quincy's logic, so long as they were indeed out of sight of the fort. Being across the river and having Porter and Redbone out there gave her comfort too. Still, it was a chilly night and the feeling of trouble wouldn't subside.

"Let's find a spot then."

It took them almost an hour to get to a spot they figured was good and sheltered, and then it took a while yet to find enough juniper to make even a tiny fire.

"I'm going to go find a little more wood," said Quincy.

Emily and Roxy continued feeding the blaze the tiny sticks they had collected along the way.

"What do you think? Is she at the fort or has she moved on?"

"What do you mean, moved on?"

"I mean do you think she is dead?"

Roxy shook her head and aware of how ratty her hair had become. She pulled a brush from her saddle bags and began brushing. 'I don't want to think about that. I guess I'm refusing to think about it, until we see a body. Grim as it is, I think they want live prisoners, you know? A dead girl doesn't do them any good."

"I'm not so sure," mumbled Emily.

"Don't talk like that," urged Roxy. "We'll get her back."

"I just worry over some things I heard, I—"

"I said to quit talking like that. You've got to stay positive in this outfit."

Emily nodded and buried her head in her knees.

Quincy returned with an armful of juniper and sage clumps. "Tain't the best wood, but it's something to keep the cold off," he said, dropping the pile beside the fire. He sat and warmed his hands. He looked at Emily then Roxy with an arched brow.

She shrugged and silently mouthed. 'She's tired.'

"Lord! We all," he said. "Sounds like they're coming back."

The sudden sound of hoofbeats made Roxy turn around with a smile. "Well that didn't take you two that long," she trailed off and the pleased grin vanished at the sight of the riders.

✳✳✳

Porter and Redbone went a good ways upriver of the fort on their side of the current before deciding to cross. It was cold. Porter wondered why he had to push himself so hard. Shouldn't life be getting easier with age? Shouldn't wisdom and being able to sit back on your laurels come at some point?

Who was he kidding? Just himself. No such luck.

His horse stepped in a hole and everyone went all the way under for just a moment. He was soaked to the bone. Redbone had fared no better with Quincy's horse.

They clambered from the river and took a moment to wring as much water out of their buckskins as possible. Then silently headed toward the route the Old Spanish Trail had carved into the desert basin. It didn't take long and they determined that Matamoros's crew had indeed passed by.

"Looks like ten horses, all right. And all of them are weighed down with extra gear or . . . prisoners."

Redbone grunted. "We are a full day behind. We must press on."

"We can only go so fast. Plus, we're down a horse. Remember?"

Redbone grunted. He got back on Quincy's bay and kicked his flanks, riding into the night following the trail.

"Stupid sum bitch," growled Porter, through his teeth.

The Ute was rapidly vanishing from sight in the moon-splashed night.

Port wanted to yell, to curse at the impetuous Ute, but he wasn't about to do anything to alert whomever was still inside the fort and might hear something in the night.

He pondered if he should chase after Redbone or go back and cut his losses. It wouldn't be right to leave Quincy and the womenfolk in the dark about all of this. They needed to know that the trail was moving on and that the fort wasn't anything they should worry about other than avoiding it.

He could still hear the faint thump of Redbone's horse's hooves as it chased after the trail splashed in moonlight. "Damn fool."

Watching the fort, Port could see the faint glow of a campfire inside. The lights flickered at the shuttered window's edges and through the gun ports in the stone walls. Yes indeed, the sooner they got away from that deathtrap the better.

Torn at what to do, Port considered chasing after Redbone at least to a point where he could holler at him to wait, lend him the horse and go and get the others. Deciding that would ultimately be the swiftest thing, he started after Redbone. But upon a slower horse, he found himself looking at the ground a bit more than the headstrong Ute. In so doing, he soon noticed a second set of prints leading back to the fort from almost the same direction.

He stopped and dismounted. Examining the tracks as closely as possible, it wasn't too hard for Port's trained eye to realize these were prints from the same animals and with that information, he walked in a wide swath until he was even sure it was the same rider's minus the weight upon one of the ten horses.

"Damn fool Ute," grumbled Porter to himself.

Scanning out at the dark horizon, Porter wondered a long moment as the wind blew in cold and cruel. Either Matamoros had killed the girl and left here out here not too far away, or they had ridden some short distance and sold the girl already. At these crossroads along the Old Spanish Trail and so close to the Navajo nation, anything was possible.

Likely as not, soon enough Redbone would spot the returning tracks and realize his impulsive mistake and come back to meet up with Porter and the others.

Port decided he better go back to the others, get some rest and wait for Redbone to return. He had to, he still needed their help against whatever foe now had his daughter, didn't he? Porter waited a long moment in the cold wind hoping he would hear Redbone doubling back but he didn't.

"Argh, horse chips," he spat, as he got back on his mount and turned back.

22. Feeling Split

Still dripping water, the gun in Matamoros' hand pointed right at Quincy.

"Where are the others? Huh? Rockwell and the Indio?" Matamoros asked. His men moved in from all round.

Roxy counted at least ten men, as she glanced about looking for any possible avenue of escape. There wasn't one.

"They're dead," said Quincy, absently.

Matamoros sneered. "If you are gonna lie to me, at least make it a good lie."

"It's the truth," insisted Emily. "The Indian was washed down the river with a bullet wound in his heart and Porter died of a snakebite." She glanced at the others as if to gain their support in her ruse.

Matamoros laughed. "She is trying, I'll give her that. But no snake could kill Rockwell, no, I think he must be scouting me out just as I am here. Eh? Good thing for me, you were foolish enough to light a fire and give me a guiding light, huh?"

"I didn't think you could see it from the fort here," said Roxy, feeling like a titanic fool.

"We couldn't, but I left Antone," he motioned to one of his Apache scouts, "on scouting duty in the hills and he came in and told me. Very bad news for you, huh?"

Quincy took an easy, slow step backward to get closer to his rifle.

"Not so fast, my negro amigo. Drop that gun belt and move a little closer. You too," he barked at Emily and Roxy. "We are gonna go back to my

Hacienda and see if maybe Rockwell doesn't return from the grave to ask after you, huh? And even if he doesn't and you were telling the truth, I have another who wants to meet you."

Emily stood up and spat.

Matamoros glared and made as if he would slap her, but Quincy intervened. "She is just a young, troubled girl, you don't need to go and get physical with her. We'll go with you. Just don't hurt them."

Matamoros gave a mirthless laugh and shook his head. "You really are crazy. Vamonos!"

The bandits picked up most of the gear and supplies, and then shoved them along heading back toward the river. They patted all of them down, but Roxy was grateful when they missed the knife strapped to her thigh. She knew she would need it sooner than later.

For the river crossing they were all bound together. Matamoros joked that if one drowned they would all drown. Roxy felt like she almost did drown in the cold waters, feeling mostly blind and bound.

On the other side, they were marched inside the fort and all placed in a small room with hay and dung on the floor. It appeared to have been a stable before their incarceration. With their hands still bound, they gingerly worked at rubbing the ropes against the rough stone of the cell, but it didn't take long for the guards to hear them. Each received a beating for the effort.

Roxy was cold, in pain and worried. Where were Porter and Redbone? Would they come charging in a hail storm of blood and thunder?

Half of her wanted them too, and the other half worried at what might happen to them if they did. A lot of people would die, maybe her and

Quincy and Emily. She looked around, hoping to see Redbone's daughter, but there didn't seem to be anyone like that here. There were several Apache warriors, a dozen Spaniards or Mexicans and a few old squaws working the more menial tasks.

Maybe they had Kimama in another room? But why keep her separate? It was a longtime until Roxy fell asleep. She seemed to think she was seeing just the hint of dawn as she passed out.

Porter was mad, but took his time crossing the river. As upset at Redbone as he was, he didn't want to risk letting whoever was in the fort know that he was out there. He dried off as best he could once again, and then headed back down to where he had left Quincy and the women.

He was more than a little irked they weren't where he had left them. It was apparent enough where they had gone through the bent grasses and sage. He knew it. They went around the hill so they could have a fire. A part of him, the cold river part, wanted the fire too, but it was risky.

He dismounted and led the stallion, now winded from two river crossings, along the path. The moon above gave little light between the clouds, just snatches making the landscape stark grey. Here and there, movement betrayed the presence of animals, coyote and ground squirrels, rabbits and night hawks, all things that hunted or were prey. Funny how each in turn was used by something else eventually. Damn, getting too introspective again, Porter told himself. Stop thinking so much about getting old and just do the job at hand. He had to tell the others about Redbone and figure out what to do, now that he knew the girl was gone again and yet there were enemies still in the fort taking potshots at whoever might cross the river. Maybe they would have to go downstream a long ways and pick up the trail again. So long as they weren't followed.

Wait, followed?

He stopped cold. A second path cut through the brush, meeting his. It was larger, as in more men had used it. He drew his Navy Colts and stepped slow and easy. Listening for anything.

Not far away he found the smoldering remains of the tiny campfire. Curious, the grass was matted down where they had been sitting. Porter could even see the prints of Quincy's coffee cup and Emily's blanket. But there was no one there and no sign of struggle. It almost looked like they had just gotten up and walked away from the campfire all on their own.

Someone had to have taken them. At least there was no blood. But damn it! Could anything go right tonight? Porter wondered, had their enemies in the fort snuck up on them, pointed their guns, and they just came freely as prisoners? He thought about that thing they'd seen last week, the Uninvited. Could that thing have mesmerized them again?

Pushing that thought out of his mind, he decided that would be too incredible a possibility to be allied with the fort. But he needed answers.

Port wheeled his stallion back off the trail and went toward the river front. Sure enough, if he strained his eyes against the black he could see some faint shambling shadows moving against the azure horizon; their forms only perceptible against the blotting out of the stars.

People were there, they had captured Quincy and the women and taken them back for some kind of unspeakable torture.

Porter cracked his knuckles. He was going to take his frustration at Redbone out on whomever had taken his friends. He'd have to deal with Redbone and Matamoros later.

Redbone's blood boiled. Why hadn't his Blood Brother followed? Wasn't he supposed to support him? They were so close now to his daughter. He could feel it. He had to hurry if he was going to save her life.

"Kimama," he said through his dry scaly lips. "Kimama, I will find you."

Racing his horse up and over the dark sage covered hills he came to a spot where a convergence of tracks caught his eye in the moonlight. Letting his horse rest a moment, he leapt down to examine the sign.

It was the same ten riders coming back to the fort. One horse might have been light a rider. Its gait and prints were softer and farther than in heading north. Perhaps his daughter had already been sold? But what if she hadn't? What if she was still back at the fort? He needed answers and, as much as it pained him, he knew he had to calm and start over. He had to go back to Porter and the others and investigate the fort.

"Great Spirit, why am I to endure these things? Why can I not just live in peace with my people? Why was my daughter taken? My sons killed? My village burned? I do not want this pain. Make my heart like a stone that I will not feel this pain anymore."

He let his prayer rise with the mist of his breath, and then he got back on his horse and rode hard toward the fort.

23. Storm is Coming

Porter was in no rush to run headlong into danger. He wanted to be the danger hunting someone else. He rode at least a mile upriver, before crossing a third time on the night. Guessing it would be best to give himself some time before spying on the fort again. He thought it best to take the long way around and truly catch the lay of the land and be wary for any outlier guards. One thing was for sure, Matamoros was twice as crafty as Porter had initially believed. The man was a snake, a cat with the nine lives, and Porter didn't much care for cats or snakes.

This side of the river had a low flat valley following the contours of the torrent between the hills. There was dry grass and a few bits of sage. The occasional juniper beside the river might give some cover if Porter snuck closer during the day; but even then, the fort had been cleared of all obstructions in every direction for at least 300 yards.

He rode back, just on the far side of the hill to the east. He intended to keep a lookout on the fort and at least see people coming or going. Taking the chance for a little bit of sleep, he soon passed out awakening only when his horse nickered softly at someone's approach.

Porter wheeled about with his six-guns drawn. It was an old Navajo wrapped in a blanket. Seeing that the man posed no threat, just curiosity, Porter lowered his guns.

The sun blazed bright yellow behind the old man. Porter realized he had slept later than he meant. He had been dog tired from all the riding and river crossings the night before. He had to be more careful. Someone a whole lot more dangerous than this old man could have snuck up on him. "Hey old-timer, you know anything about that fort?"

The old Indian nodded slowly, but gestured for food instead of giving answers. Porter got up and found a piece of hardtack in his saddlebags. He broke it in half handing the old man the smaller half for breakfast.

The old man babbled, pointing toward the fort and then at Porter's half of the hardtack. Not following what the old man was saying, Porter nodded, and offered the larger half in his left hand instead of the smaller half in his right hand. The old man shook his head and took both pieces of the hardtack.

"Fine, but I hope you have something to tell me that is worthwhile," grumbled Porter.

The old man put both pieces of the hardtack in the satchel at his side. He then pointed toward the fort, saying, "Much bad medicine there. The Stag-Man takes people."

"Stag-Man?"

The old man nodded. "Witch. Brujo. The Mexicans sell him slaves." He repeated earnestly.

All of Porter's fears about the Uninvited came flooding back. He knew there was good in the world, but for every bit of light there was dark to contrast that brightness. How it all worked, he sure had no idea, but he respected it was indeed there. But, he couldn't focus on any of that philosophizing, this problem was flesh and blood down there in the fort.

"You wouldn't know any way for me to get in there without them knowing, would you?"

The old man shook his head again, "No."

"Anybody passing through today, you think?"

"No."

"All right, if you had to get in there what would you do?"

The old man grinned. For a moment, Porter thought he had an answer, but then he said, "I wouldn't go."

"Thanks, you've been a heap of help."

The old man gave a chuckle saying, "You have a heap big problem."

Porter shook his head.

The old man seemed to ponder a moment, he scratched his ears and looked away to the northwest. "Maybe if you help the Diné. We give you help."

"Yeah, what's that?"

"Make crazy horses and you give me fort."

Porter furrowed his brow. "How exactly are you going to do that? Do you mean their horses down there?" Even at this distance he could see at least ten horses penned beside the fort.

The old Indian shook his head with a grin. "No, those are my horses. But I can help you, if you give me fort." He beckoned for Porter to follow him.

"Help me get my friends and, yes, you can have the fort."

Thinking this was a fool errand from a crazy old man, Porter grudgingly followed, leading his horse. They walked up and down few gullies and back up a steep rise of jagged rock and scrambled up over the top. When they reached the zenith, Porter stopped in amazement.

The old man pointed, saying, "Crazy horses."

Spread out below them was small village, but with a massive herd of horses grazing all about it. There were hundreds. It was quite a sight in the early mornings light.

"Crazy horses riding everywhere," said the old man with pride.

Porter took off his hat in astonishment. "You old fox. You didn't need my hardtack, you're a king out here."

The old man beamed.

"When can we do your distraction?"

"Dusk."

"I don't like waiting that long to help my friends, but I suppose it will have to do."

✲✲✲

It was midafternoon when a familiar face rode up to Porter and the old man as they sat upon the hill.

"Redbone. Glad, you came back," said Porter. "This here is—"

But Redbone didn't let him finish before he snapped, "Why didn't you come with me?"

Porter stood, agitated, remembering all the anger and frustration he felt the night before at Redbone's impetuous chase. "You damn fool, you could'a waited for the rest of us. If you hadn't been so hard-headed you would have noticed sooner that the riders double backed."

"Without my daughter!"

"We don't know that. Even if they did, we need to find out who they sold her too."

Redbone fumed and made as if he would strike out at Porter, but the long-haired gunfighter leaned in as if expecting it.

The old man intervened. "Good men need to help one another, not fight when the dark ways rise. Much darkness down there. No fight ourselves."

"He's right," grumbled Porter.

Redbone relented and stepped back. He grumbled and sat down a few paces away. "I cannot wait forever."

"And we aren't going to. Chief Dan here says there is a lot of bad medicine involved and we need all the help we can get. Him and his boys are going to give us a distraction to get down there and raise some hell. It's risky but it's all we've got. Ain't no cavalry coming but us."

"Cavalry? No, blue coats, no good." Redbone said, with his hand making a chopping motion.

"My mistake. It's a figure of speech, let it go."

Redbone rubbed at his sore jaw and held out his empty canteen. Porter nodded and tossed him his. "We got a deal going. We take care of whoever is inside and let Chief Dan here keep the fort as he sees fit."

"But it is on Ute land."

"Navajo," countered Chief Dan.

"We need his help. I don't give a damn whose land you think it is, right now for the help it's going to the Navajo."

Redbone clearly didn't like the deal, but he nodded. "Navajo."

✱✱✱

Sunlight peeked through the open chinks in the stone, and wind gave a cool bit of breath into what was otherwise a stifling chamber. Roxy looked around. The others were awake, but sitting quietly propped up against the walls.

"Thought I'd let you sleep. I figured it was good if at least one of us could," said Quincy.

"I don't think I fell asleep til dawn. Too much worry."

"I hear you," said Quincy. He subtly motioned for Roxy to steal a glance.

One of the Mexican bandits stood nearby and was not subtly trying to listen from just to the side of the threshold. Quincy held up a hand with two fingers, signaling there were two men on each side of the threshold.

Roxy nodded and held up her bound hands with a wistful look. She silently mouthed that she still had her thigh dagger.

Quincy chuckled, and whispered, "You're right. I almost forgot they got us trussed up like turkeys. Still, I want to be ready. We know the long-hair is gonna come with guns blazing."

"That's what I'm afraid of."

They heard Matamoros coming closer, speaking to one of his men. "Look, now that we have her back, he can have both the blondie and this redhead too. I think Senor Mala Cosa will like them very much. We can probably ask for double. Yes?"

The fat bandit with Matamoros had cartridge belts slung crisscross over his body. A scar over his left eye gave him a lazy, yet sly, demeanor. He grinned lasciviously at Emily. "Maybe, she should stay with me here. I would pay you."

Matamoros, who had seemed almost amiable just a moment before, flew into a rage. "Are you mad? I already delayed in giving Mala Cosa what he wanted once, I can't do that again. He wants the blondie, he gets the blondie."

The fat man backed away, but then puffed out his chest. "You are so afraid of this Mala Cosa. I am not!"

"Because you know nothing!" countered Matamoros. "He has dark powers. You are better off not knowing, you great fool!"

The fat man scowled and struck one his underlings standing guard at the door. "I am not afraid, no matter what you say," he bellowed, but then stormed off so he couldn't be stuck in the tirade.

Matamoros stuck his head inside the chamber and leered a long moment. "We have great plans for you, my friends. Great plans. I will redeem myself with you." Then he was gone.

"What did he mean redeem himself with us? Is he going to let us go?" asked Emily wiping a tear from her eye.

Roxy shook her head, and blew a piece of straw that dangled from her hair away. "No. He means to sell us to someone he owes a favor too, to get back in their good graces."

"Oh." The single word tumbled from the girl's mouth, pushed out by a head full of despair.

Quincy craned his neck to look through a gun port behind him. He saw the bright sunlight and rolling hills of the high desert. "A storm is coming. Porter will bring the blood and thunder just you wait. We'll get out of this."

24. Crazy Horses Riding Everywhere

The waiting dragged on forever as the sun ticked across the sky. Finally, Chief Dan said it was time. His sons were guiding the herd around the bend far to the south of the fort. Once they crossed over the hills, they would get the horses running alongside the river in a mad thunder. It was dangerous, but the chaos, dust and confusion would grant a semblance of concealment, if not cover, for Porter and Redbone to get close to the fort. Then the hard part would begin.

Porter hoped his friends were still alive and in decent health. Hard to say what Matamoros might have done to them at this point. Considering he hadn't killed them outright back at the camp, well, Porter was going to take that as a good sign, at least as good a sign as could be expected out in this cursed, strange land.

Porter and Redbone mounted their own horses, but let themselves be overtaken by Chief Dan's herd. Hundreds of horses moved across the valley, bringing the drumming of hooves with clouds of dust in their wake.

Chief Dan chanted a song in his own tongue and beat a drum, while also waving a smoking branch of sage. That he could stay in the saddle while doing it all was testament to what a fine horseman he was.

Porter rode up beside him and asked, "What are you singing?"

"I am sending a message to the good spirits, to guide and protect us and the Crazy Horses."

Porter just looked at him.

"They like the song too," said Chief Dan.

The herd moved in unison now at a fast trot. Even the clouds overhead seemed to be moving faster than usual and a cool breeze waved in their favor. Despite the crazed chaotic plan, Porter had a good feeling about it. Chief Dan's song seemed to rally a whole lot of good will into everything.

"When we get closer, we will go faster," said Chief Dan, with a wild grin. "More thunder, more dust, more crazy!"

Porter could barely see the fort rising in the distance ahead of the herd. The Chief's sons urged the animals on and the body moved faster and faster. The ground reverberated with the constant pounding of hooves.

* * *

Inside the fort, everyone heard the dull thud like a giant's steps approaching. The bandits watched out the windows and gun ports and shouted in amazement and fear.

"There are a bunch of crazy horses running toward us!"

"Eh?" gasped Matamoros, going to look for himself. "Ay yiyi. Dios mio. What is happening?"

In their makeshift cell, Roy, Quincy and Emily felt the tremor of the horses' approach and heard the wild neigh of the herd coming closer.

"Didn't I say he would bring the thunder?" said Quincy.

The dust choked them, but Porter and Redbone both gritted their teeth, spat and kept their heads down. The herd raced past the fortress and gunfire sounded from the bandits, attempting to scare the horses away.

There were far too many of Chief Dan's crazy horses for them all to be persuaded to move away or killed, the stampede of so many behind kept a steady flow rumbling past.

Porter and Redbone became separated in the confusion. Redbone found himself beside the fort and he leapt from his saddle to the sod roof. He drew his tomahawk and pistol, and ran over the top until he was looking down into the courtyard.

There were at least a half-dozen of the Mexican bandits and Apache within the courtyard, but they were all looking out the windows at the horses. How they missed spotting him, he never knew. He took careful aim at three of the bandits crowded together, guessing that while his marksmanship was not the best, he would still hit them.

Opening fire failed to cause as much chaos as he expected. Between their own firing at the horses and the incredible dull roar, three men fell dead or wounded before any of the others noticed they were being attacked.

When a bandit did notice, he shouted to his compadres that an Indian was on the roof. Without time to reload, Redbone did the insane thing and threw his empty pistol at the bandit to throw off his aim. As the man ducked, Redbone leapt to the courtyard with his bowie knife and tomahawk. He caved in the bandit's skull then ran at the next man, tearing him asunder. He dodged the last bandit's wicked aim with a rifle and sunk his tomahawk into the bandit's neck. With all his foes dead, he rushed inside urgently searching for Kimama.

Reaching a small chamber, Redbone saw Roxy, Quincy and Emily inside. He cautiously entered, then cut Roxy's bonds, and started on Quincy's. Before he could finish, or get to Emily, a bandit shot into the chamber and they all threw themselves against the walls to avoid being hit.

"Where is Porter? Can you get me a gun?" shouted Quincy, over the din, still waving his bound hands.

Redbone shook his head, holding up his only two weapons.

Quincy cursed, still feeling useless in the fray.

Porter made it to the fort, but despite the chaos he was spotted. Bandits fired at him and his horse spooked and bucked him off. He tumbled into the dirt amidst the stamping hooves of scores of horses. Clouds of dust granted some concealment, but no cover from the flying lead. A horse screamed and tumbled over beside him in its death throes.

He rolled, got up and threw himself against the fort's stone wall. A bandit stuck his pistol out a small gun port to reach around the side and shoot Porter, but the wily gunslinger grabbed the man's arm, pulled and broke it, while disarming his foe. Pointing it back into the gun port, where he still held the trapped arm, he shot the bandit with his own gun.

Waiting for a brief respite from the swarm of lead, Porter ran around the side of the fort, hunting for another way in. He knew that this place wouldn't be quite as hard to get through as the traditional forts of the Americans. These were of stacked stone with multiple windows and great beams to support the roof and at times, keep the walls from settling and falling. It was a precarious balance where settling of the foundation occurred.

After shooting another bandit that leaned too far out one of the windows, Porter went and crawled through the same.

Inside the courtyard, a quick, furious gunfight made the bandits retreat. They closed big double doors and sealed off the rest of the fort from Porter's position.

He brainstormed what he could do. A beam was planted against the wall over the doorway and stretched out almost twelve feet to the outside wall. Porter looped a rope about the beam and tossed it to Chief Dan who had just ridden up outside.

The old man nodded, looped the rope about his saddle and had his mount pull away, forcing a big section of the stacked wall to come down. The tumbled walls also freed one of the doors which lurched onto its side.

Amid the ruckus, two bandits rushed in with guns blazing, but were met by Porter's lead. They fell down wounded, only to get their skulls crushed by the last couple falling stones. Porter slipped inside the fort, pushing through the gap where the two had come from.

✳✳✳

Hearing a terrible commotion on the opposite end of the fort, the shooting let up just enough for Redbone to rush out and chop into another of the bandits. He glanced about for a gun to arm Quincy, but saw nothing but the pistol the dead bandit had. Reaching for it he heard a semi-familiar cackle behind him. Matamoros and the fat captain stood a dozen paces away. Each had their guns leveled at him and could have shot and killed him in an instant.

"You had to come back for more, eh Indio? I will teach you to stay down," sneered Matamoros.

A pair of bandits rushed in, jabbering about Porter being outside.

"Then go deal with him! Don't let him in, you idiots. Kill him!"

Returning his attention back to Redbone, Matamoros grinned and holstered his pistol, then drew his saber. "Now Indio, just you and me with our blades, eh?"

Redbone was encouraged. He didn't like that there were four bandits watching him with their guns drawn, but he felt confident he could kill this slaver snake with his tomahawk and knife, even if the saber had a greater reach.

They circled each other once in the courtyard. Redbone he had fought many men in just such a situation and only one to what he considered a draw. The others were dead. He leapt in quick, swinging the tomahawk wide and thrusting with the knife, but Matamoros was quicker. He slashed

Redbone across the wrist and danced back just out of reach of the two strikes.

Redbone was astonished at the Mexican's speed. He suddenly felt like he was the one being toyed with.

Matamoros taunted, "Again, Indio. Try again."

Redbone wiped his bleeding wrist beneath his arm, but it did not staunch the flow. His hand was becoming too slick to hold the knife with a sure grip. Gambling on another attack, Redbone threw the tomahawk. It spun, like wheeling death.

But Matamoros dodged aside.

The tomahawk buried itself in a man behind Matamoros and the bandit chieftain laughed as the man died.

"You see that?"

The fat captain looked at him in disgust, but Matamoros shrugged, saying, "He shouldn't have been standing there."

Switching the knife to his unwounded hand, Redbone came in again. Intent on killing this most hated of enemies, he silently charged. But Matamoros again danced away, teasing the Ute, and slapping him on the back with the flat of his blade.

"Are we almost done?"

Redbone said nothing, returning to his usual stony expression, hiding pain and worry.

Matamoros stepped in and slashed a retreating Redbone across the stomach. Redbone crashed to his knees, as the howling pain and blood spilled from him. Then just to be cruel, Matamoros gave him another gash across his other arm and then a wicked cut across his cheek.

"You see? I can count coup too."

The sound of the horse stampede was dying away, since the herd had nearly all passed on down the valley and the desert returned to its natural state. Even the dust clouds had drifted on, but an eruption of sudden gunfire, took out the fat captain and an Apache scout who had been standing beside him.

Matamoros wheeled to see Porter inside the fortress. Porter's gun was aimed at his chest. Porter grinned and pulled the trigger. It went click. His face dropped.

"Aw, horse chips." He ducked back through the doorway to reload.

"Hey, Gringo. You better stop being so unfriendly if you want your friends to live. I have more guns than you, with bullets, and they are all pointed here at your friends. Come on out and we can talk about settling this to the death, just me and you."

Porter stepped through the threshold. "Guess it's my lucky day then."

25. Blades

Redbone lay on the ground, bleeding out from his wounds. The slash across his wrist was spurting blood while his stomach wounds puddled at his feet. He was growing faint.

"Someone put some pressure on those wounds or he won't make it," growled Porter.

"So you are next gringo," taunted Matamoros. "You saw what I just did to your amigo, what do you think I will do to you? The pendejo Indio I could respect, but you?" He spat. "I don't even like you."

Porter patted the butt of his six-shooter. "You want to duel? Let's duel."

Matamoros laughed, but shouted to his men to be sure that they had their rifles trained both on Porter and the others. "I won't play your games. I have heard how deadly you are with a gun. If we are going to play games, we will play mine. My rules, my weapons. Drop that gun belt or my men will shoot all of your friends."

Porter looked around. There were too many men, too many guns leveled at Roxy, Emily, Quincy, and even the incapacitated Redbone, let alone himself. People would die. The bandidos grinned and laughed wickedly, as if they hoped Porter would try just so they could shoot his friends.

"We're gonna duel then?"

Matamoros nodded.

"All right," said Porter, letting his gun belt drop.

"Porter, no," pleaded Roxy. "Don't worry about us, kill him!"

Matamoros smiled like a cat with a mouse between its claws. Porter knew he had something up his sleeve but what?

"No one can say that I didn't give the infamous Mormon gringo a chance. I don't want anybody saying I shot you in the back or something. No, they will fear my name more than yours, once I kill you. But you and I, we will fight my way. Diego!"

The bandit Matamoros had shouted at vanished for a brief moment then came back with another saber. He offered it to Matamoros.

"Porter," called Roxy. "Don't. He beat Redbone faster than I could see."

"With what? That pig-sticker?"

Roxy vigorously nodded.

Matamoros's grin widened, if that was even possible. "I see that you are a man not easily frightened. I like that." His visage darkened. "But I am going to cut your heart out and feed it to you."

"Whatever you say, Estupido."

Matamoros reddened, as if a feverish storm cloud flew across his face, but he drew in quick breaths through his flaring nostrils and calmed himself. "There was a time when that would have upset me. You are a very rude person saying that to a man like me, and you will pay with blood!"

"I wouldn't have it any other way."

"We fight with these," said Matamoros, tossing the saber at Porter's feet.

"You want to fight me with that?" drawled Porter in contempt.

Matamoros nodded, flashing his eyes in triumph as he swished his blade through the air in a figure eight at incredible speed.

"Am I supposed to be impressed?"

"You ought to be, Gringo. I am the best swordsman in all of Mexico! During the revolution, I cut down five of Maximillian's best bodyguard in a row! They were French, the best Napoleon the third had to offer to defend his puppet."

"Who?" teased Porter.

"I know what you are trying to do, Gringo, and it won't work."

Porter snickered. "So, you want me to pick up this piece of pig iron and fight you? Like pirates?"

"Like men!" shouted Matamoros, indignant.

"All right, hold on." Porter put on his roping gloves. Thick cowhide meant for when he was working the range.

Matamoros grinned wickedly, guessing Porter thought he would be defending his hands from the quick slashes he could inflict, just as he had so recently done to Redbone's exposed flesh.

Porter flexed his hands within the gloves, stretching the fingers in and out. He then picked up the saber with his right hand. He swished it through the air back and forth getting a feel for the blade. "It ain't my kind of weapon, but I suppose it will get the job done."

Matamoros laughed. "I'm glad you think so." He brought his blade up. It captured sunlight across the razor-sharp edge, dazzling the sight of all present.

Porter however stuck the tip of his blade in the ground and casually danced the tip through the dirt as if he were signing his name.

"What are you doing? You are disgracing that blade. It was forged in Toledo!"

"Ohio?"

"Spain!"

"Fine," drawled Porter absently. "I just thought I'd write you a message before I kill you."

"What?" snapped Matamoros. "A message in the dirt? You're loco Gringo. Absolutely loco."

Porter continued sweeping the tip of the saber back and forth in the dirt.

Matamoros stepped closer, curious. His blade was up and at the ready to parry any sudden move on Porter's part.

But the gunfighter kept his blade tip down in the dirt continuing his meandering scrawl.

"I cannot read those scratches. I'll just kill you now if you will not defend yourself."

"Just read it," insisted Porter.

Matamoros kept his blade up and at the ready. Even with a swift swordsman, he was closer to being able to cross blades than someone who had their point down and in the dirt. Porter couldn't possibly be fast enough to cut him. Not against the fastest swordsman in all of Mexico.

Porter's left hand shot out and grabbed Matamoros saber about a third of the way down the blade.

The bandit chief's eyes went wide with shock. Sudden fear gripped him as strong as Porter's own hand. He tried but he could not pull the saber from Porters grasp. "No! Gringo! No!"

Porter raised his own blade and brought it down like a thunderbolt across Matamoros's neck.

The bandit's cries were lost, even as his lips still moved. His head nearly came clean off. It flopped down on his chest as a red wave gushed. Somehow his sombrero stayed on.

Dumbstruck, the bandido's collective mouths dropped. Some reacted with violence, some fled.

Now armed with two blades, Porter flung the left one at the nearest bandit, throwing off his shocked aim, as he cut him down.

Quincy dove for Porter's gun belt and started firing, just as the bandits returned same.

The bandits shrieked in terror. It was an uproar, a crazed, bewildering nightmare of Porter coming at them with deadly Toledo steel and lead flying.

Roxy wrapped up Redbone's wounds while Emily struggled to work her own bonds free.

Quincy kept firing until the six-gun was empty. With his hands tied he couldn't very well reload but he sure tried.

Porter stormed after the bandits like a mad dog with the bloody sword. He cut down one bandit as he turned to level his pistol.

Another cried out as he found his escape cut off. Porter's mercy was gone.

One man leapt to escape out a window and was stuck thru between the shoulder blades for his troubles.

An Apache rifleman fired at Porter from around a corner. He ducked back but didn't see the mad gunman anymore. The dead Mexican in the window was the only sign of anyone having just been there. Backing away, the Apache glanced behind and then forward again. He knew death was close.

He stepped to where the horses were corralled. A sound caught his ears and as he looked forward he saw a flying sword that took him in the head.

Porter charged and took the Apache's rifle.

One bandit was making good his escape on horseback. Porter leveled the rifle and took aim.

"Wait," said Quincy. "We need one alive. We need to know where they took the girl."

"What are you talking about," growled Porter.

"They sold the girl, she isn't here," responded Quincy.

Porter lowered his aim and shot the horse out from under the fleeing bandit.

The man went flying and hit the earth in a cloud of dust.

Porter halfway hoped the man hadn't broken his neck in the fall.

He went after the man just in case the bandit could get up and run.

Porter walked up on the man cautious, in case he might roll over and shoot, but there was no danger of that. His neck was twisted at bizarre crooked angle and he wouldn't be rolling over anywhere except in hell.

Searching the man's pockets, Porter found nothing to indicate anywhere the man might have been hoping to get to. It had just been a blind panic to escape. He didn't even have a canteen. Porter took the dead man's gun belt and strode back to the fort.

The others were now free of their bindings. Roxy and Quincy were doing what they could for Redbone, but it didn't look good for the old Indian.

Quincy was the first to speak, especially noticing Porter had not returned with the escaping man. "Did you kill him?"

Porter shrugged, and said while thumbing behind himself, "Yeah. Broke his neck."

"We needed him Port! We don't know who or where they took Redbone's daughter. How are we supposed to find them? Our tracker isn't up to tracking no more. He might not make it."

"Pull back your reins, Quint. I can track," growled Porter.

"Not as good as Redbone, you can't, Yankee! 'Sides you said it had to be him that rescued his own daughter anyhow. And, if he lives, he won't be up to no rough travel."

"We'll find a way. Quit being such a damn pessimist, Quint!"

Emily spoke up. "I might have an idea of where they went."

"Well?" snapped Roxy, surprised.

"When my sisters and I were prisoners, I understood a little of what Matamoros's men were talking about. They kept saying that they were going to sell us to a Senor Mala Cosa, a Mr. Bad Thing? I don't know who that was or what they meant by that. They did say that he was residing near some ruins."

"Ruins? Did they mention which ruins? This landscape is littered with ruins."

"Throw a rock out here and you'll hit somebody's ruins," said Quincy.

"They might have mentioned a square tower."

Porter shook his head. "Not enough to go on. I can think of at least four."

"They said something about it being north of the winged rock and one said needle point."

Porter grinned. "Now we're getting somewhere. That's the sacred mountain of the Diné."

"Diné?"

"That's what the Navajo call themselves. It means 'the people'. But, the Winged Rock, that's the big striking mountain not too far south from here. You can see it when we get out of this valley. The important thing though is that we're close. Those square tower ruins are due north of us."

"How far?"

"Hard to say, this desert is rough going. Easier if we stick by the river and we'll have water, but we don't know how long whoever has the girl will stick around that place. Maybe they'll be moving on real soon."

"We have to try," said Roxy.

"Course we do, I'm just wondering if some of us should stay and some of us should hurry it along."

"What's that mean?" Roxy snapped.

"It means, somebody stays here to look after a wounded Redbone and I go after the—,"

"Kidnappers," suggested Quincy.

"Kidnappers," said Porter.

"I'm not just going to hang around here feeling useless. I am going with you—to help."

"Useless? Looking after those in need is helping. And needed badly."

"The hell you say."

"The hell I do say! Little Sister, you've got a gift of caring those that are injured, I've got a gift for making people injured, do the math and let's do what we do best!"

She crossed her arms frowning, but there was no verbal argument. Porter nodded at her, hoping there was an understanding, but the back of his mind itched that this wasn't over.

The moon rose as darkness fell and everyone slept as hard as they had in ages.

26. Tracking

The next morning, Chief Dan and his sons arrived after having gathered back their crazy horse herd. They took over the fort and began by clearing out the dead. He chanted his songs and burned sage to purify the place, but it didn't take very long before he said he wasn't sure it could be purified and it was a good thing the bad men had been killed and driven out and that was the end of it.

Porter and Quincy made sure their horses were fed, watered and brushed down. They then prepared provisions, especially water.

Quincy noticed the section of wall that had come down. "How the hell did that happen? The stampede?"

Porter shrugged, but Chief Dan answered. "The hairy man did it. He could find no other way in." His sons glanced at each other in surprise.

"He did what? How?" He shouted at Porter, "Maybe you do got a Samson thing going."

Porter nodded and mounted his horse.

"Little Sister, you've got this. It's an important job. Tell you what. If Redbone is feeling patched up enough that he can be moved, we will leave some markers along our trail you can't miss. Remember we're heading almost due north, but will have to do some zig-zagging on account of ravines. Always keep your eyes skinned for trouble. But, if Redbone gets a fever and is delirious, you better stay put."

Roxy scrunched up her face, cursed and stalked off.

"What'd I say?"

Quincy shook his head. "Don't ask," he laughed. "We best get moving."

They rode alongside the river for several miles. When it switched back running westward, they continued straight ahead north into the bleak desert.

They left a marker of stacked stones, just in case Roxy and the others followed, but Redbone appeared to be in bad enough shape that Porter didn't think he would be able to ride for days.

By late afternoon, they were well into rolling grass and sage-covered hills where, every now and again, a section of stone would loom out showing the beginnings of a ravine or small canyon. Porter examined these entrances and deemed that no one had passed through them. He also found sign of where the men of Matamoros had passed by earlier to sell the girl. But with shifting sands and hard rock sometimes he would also lose the trail.

"If I didn't have a pretty good idea on where they were heading already, this would be a mighty frustrating task."

"I believe," said Quincy. "Now, once we find this Mala Cosa, what then? How many men do you think he might have?"

"I have no idea, but I didn't want the trail to get too cold, and we don't want him killing the girl if we can stop him."

"You think it will come to that? You think we're running out of time?"

"Maybe. I don't know my constellations as well as some, but I fear that something might happen when the moon is full. Like tonight."

"Convenient."

"Tell me about it. It's always a full moon when some dark things take place and people go crazy."

"You been around a lot of dark things and crazy people before?"

147

"You could say that's a fair assessment, yeah."

Stars popped into existence within the deep azure sky and the moon rose in the east from behind the great mesas. The wind was still and a feeling of cold more than actual temperature struck them as they rode up on a bewitching little canyon. It gouged itself into the table of land like a festering wound and great dark rocks were jumbled about like healing scabs.

"I take it this is the place?"

"Don't say that to me," snorted Porter.

"How you want to do this?"

"Well, riding right up there is a death trap."

"Agreed," said Quincy. "Course everything has been a death trap on this trip."

"But I believe the girl is in there and the trail leads in there."

"Uh-huh. I don't like where this is going."

Porter turned in the saddle, saying "I'll ride in slow and easy, giving you time to go up on the left and be over watch with your rifle."

"Split up? And me up there?" He said, pointing on the ridge.

"Yeah, you'll be my guardian angel."

"Guardian angel? You're the Destroying Angel, what you need me for?" Quincy said, with a chuckle. But he tipped his hat and started riding up the left-hand side.

27. Drums in the Night

The mouth of the canyon beckoned Porter to enter like a spider welcomes the fly. The red-brown stones that had tumbled from the entrance reminded him of teeth. He couldn't help but wonder if these jaws were about to snap shut, but a hero has to do what only he can, and Port knew he was the only one who could ride in and out of this alive.

Porter held off riding in until Quincy was on top of the table land and could effectively see ahead. Somewhere an owl hooted. Letting his stallion slowly trot in, Porter watched every boulder and shadow for movement that might betray an ambush. He thought something moved ahead in the darkness, but he couldn't see what it was. Waiting a long moment, he determined it could not have been a man and so it should not have been a danger.

Glancing up toward Quincy, the buffalo soldier didn't seem aware of anything yet either. When he was at least a quarter mile in, Porter thought he heard the soft mutter of drums. A trick of the night made him think he could see the flickering, dancing glow of flames from somewhere far up the canyon.

He caught sight of Quincy and the buffalo soldier signaled all clear. Porter signaled back and continued a slow, easy trot through the canyon. There was a trail moving through the clary sage, but it was hard packed and might have been there for ages untold.

Red ruins of some ancient castles squatted about either side of the canyon. They were made of red brick, stacked high and tight, but with an occasional window or door that made them look like grinning skulls in the darkness. Port kept his eyes skinned for trouble, any hint of enemies, but there was no sign of anyone except perhaps ghosts dwelling in those stone houses.

Keeping an eye out for Quincy, Porter saw no sign of his friend who had already dismounted. He decided it might be wisest if he did the same. Porter climbed off his horse and lightly wrapped the reins about a sage. The animal would have no issue freeing itself if it put its mind to it. But for now, if Porter had to run, his horse would be nearby.

The drums were louder now, pounding, and a long drawn out cry of horror and agony suddenly echoed through the canyon.

With his Colt .45 drawn, Porter picked up his pace. He made his way around the bend, each footfall revealed a little more of the glow of the fire and the throb of the drums.

High above on his right was the largest of the ruins, outlined against the starry night. Several rounded towers were etched against the star filled night. As he reached the last bend, it was the curious square tower straight ahead that most captured his attention.

A blazing bonfire in front of the tower lit up the canyon and reflected off the red monolith. A rough stone altar was prepared across from the flames and a dark figure moved with malevolent abandon.

Porter noticed the scent of decay about him. Bones of man and beast were strewn here and there. The voice cried out again and directed his attention from the death underfoot to that which loomed ahead, Porter pressed on.

"This time, you came willingly into my abode," thundered a voice from the flames.

Despite still being shrouded in the darkness, the man saw Porter, and Porter saw him.

Horror! It was the Uninvited. He looked much the same, dressed in rags, greasy, gray hair that stood out wildly, the penetrating stink of death and those wicked, inhuman black eyes.

A girl with dark hair struggled on the altar, Kimama, Redbone's daughter. Her face was black and blue from beatings, her clothes torn and ripped.

"Too long, you have kept me from what is mine."

Porter watched the ridge, hoping to catch some sign of Quincy, but saw nothing. He didn't see any one in support of the Uninvited either, but he still didn't put his guard or his pistol down.

"You stole sacrifices that belonged to me. Matamoros was bringing me much blood."

Porter stepped closer, keeping his pistol trained on the Uninvited. "I ain't sorry to disappoint a demon."

The Uninvited gave a smirk and stepped aside the fire to come closer. "They are coming, your friends. I can see it. I will covenant with all of your blood. You came willingly, they will come willingly. Put down your weapon."

"Like Hell," growled Porter. But staring into those bottomless black eyes weakened something in Porter's resolve. Some spell, some enchantment gripped Porter, and he unwillingly lowered his weapon.

"I will feast on her, you and your friends, just like I have on all the others that fall into my domain."

It was them that Porter realized the horror of how many bodies were strewn about the area. The cast off remains of dozens was piled into corners and crevices. Then to his revolting surprise, some of the corpses stood up.

"My children," said the Uninvited, motioning to the half dozen shambling figures.

"So, you're Senor Mala Cosa?" Porter asked.

"Some call me that," said the sorcerer. "I have many names in this country."

Porter struggled to bring his gun to bear, to spare the world from this cannibal sorcerer, but his guts failed him. He doubled over in disgust and pain, pummeling him from some unknown abysmal gulf.

"My power is greatest here in my home, where you," Mala Cosa pointed a finger accusingly, "are the uninvited." The horde of dark skeletal figures ambled forth in a rotten mockery of life. "My sons will feast upon your flesh and my daughters will wear your long scalp."

Six grim figures with faces painted like death stepped closer. Younger than Mala Cosa, they each held his foul reek. Hands with fingers like claws scoured over Porter, tearing at him. He couldn't fight back, just survive their attack.

A shot rang out. One of the son's eyes rolled up as the bullet took the top of his skull. The others backed away staring into the darkness.

"There on the edge!" cried Mala Cosa, pointing at the ridge where Quincy lay.

Strange cries erupted from dank spider-haunted corners, and Porter could only guess that there were more of Mala Cosa's children than had initially been revealed.

The brief distraction brought Porter's will back. He raised his pistol and shot one of the ghouls in the chest, then another and another. The rest scattered but Quincy fired at them too and they dropped in death throes.

Then Quincy was crying out as white and black skeletal forms assaulted his position on the ridge. Porter was on his own in the canyon.

Wave after wave of leering hungry mouths came at Porter. When he ran out of ammunition, he drew his blessed Bowie knife. The horde came on with a wailing and gnashing of teeth. Porter went to town on them like he was cutting like hogs at market.

✳✳✳

Quincy shot a half dozen attackers, then, as they crawled through the tumbled stone bricks of the ruin, he bashed them with his rifle like a club. Until there were no more. He quickly reloaded and gingerly looked about.

One reared up and bit at his leg, Quincy put the end of the barrel to its skull and fired. A terrible wailing ruckus echoed in the canyon so he scrambled out to see. Porter was there cutting down two dozen of the skeletal monsters. The sight of it made even a veteran like Quincy aghast.

✳✳✳

More than a dozen mangled bodies were spread out before Porter and still more of the walking demons came. He bashed one aside only to have another take its place. The wave of gruesome kept coming until Port cut the wolf inside loose and brought the attack to them. A frenzied mound of death grew at his feet as the bodies piled up. He roared at them and for an instant the demons faltered.

A stone struck Porter and he reeled away. One of the last sons held a spear about to skewer Porter, when a gunshot took the death mask between the eyes and he fell backward.

Quincy, waved, then looked for any other attackers. Seeing none, he scrambled down the slope to assist Porter on the canyon floor.

Catching his breath with a reprieve from the onslaught, Porter found a spare cylinder for his Colt .45 loaded it and brought it to bear. Mala Cosa stood beside the fire, holding Kimama with an obsidian dagger to her delicate throat. While he was disturbed at what had been done to his clan, he would not give up.

Quincy came racing up with his rifle at the ready. He stared at Porter in revulsion. His friend was covered in gore. But, Porter didn't notice, in this moment he was focused solely on Mala Cosa.

"You and your friend will leave my valley. You will forget you were ever here. You will not remember this place. You will forget. Leave!"

Quincy blinked and immediately retched. The very suggestion brought him to his knees. Sickness clenched his guts and he wasn't sure he could breathe if he didn't get away from this demon in human form. He scrambled back and away.

"You must obey me," said Mala Cosa.

Taken to his knees, Porter was equally struck and the pistol faltered in his hand, drooping and pointing at the ground though his trigger finger still held the gun.

"You will end your own life!"

Shaking uncontrollably, Porter brought his gun up toward his own head. The barrel shook in his hand. Sweat poured down his face. His thumb pulled back the hammer.

"You cannot resist my power!" thundered Mala Cosa.

The girl, trapped between the mad man and his knife cried out, powerless to escape his wicked grasp. It was enough of a distraction to put a hairline fracture in the sorcerer's sinister urge.

That tiny spark of disruption, granted the briefest respite for Porter's resistance and he broke through the enchantment.

Porter grasped the barrel of his pistol and threw it with all the force he could muster at Mala Cosa's face.

The sorcerer pushed the girl aside and tried to block the flying gun with his knife.

Wheeling through the air, the gun pointed death in an arc of doom. Until it connected. The obsidian blade shattered at the gun's impact.

With Mala Cosa's concentrated mesmerism broken, Porter was up and rejuvenated in an instant. He leapt and tackled Mala Cosa, pummeling the sorcerer before he could utter another spellbinding word.

Quincy gathered himself and took in the gruesome scene. "Let's get outta here."

Porter rained a few more blows on the sorcerer until the dirty man stopped moving.

"I think you've got him," said Quincy.

Porter looked at his friend with eyes ablaze. Quincy stepped back in fear.

"I ain't never had anyone get into my head like that. It ain't happening again."

"Did you kill him?" Quincy asked.

"No."

"Then why don't we just shoot him here and now?"

Porter shook his head. "No, this scum is going to atone for his crimes. We are going to find out how many lives perished at his hands. We take him alive and get answers."

"Who us?"

"No, lawyers, judges, and newspapermen, anyone with more skills at words than I have. More people must know about this. I expect lots of folks are wanting answers about loved ones who never came home."

They bound Mala Cosa up with the ropes that had been holding Kimama. They also tied a bandana around his mouth then found a sack to cinch over his head. They dragged him out of the canyon and up the hill to make a camp. No one could stand to stay the night in that bloody canyon.

"Port, what were all those things? Men? Or demons?"

Porter shrugged. "I don't know. I guess they could have been a bit of both."

"I don't want to ever talk about this night again," Quincy said, tossing some twigs on the fire.

✳✳✳

In the morning, they began back, but were surprised and overjoyed to find Roxy leading a horse with Redbone slumped over it. Emily, Chief Dan and a pair of his sons followed behind the pair.

"He couldn't wait to come for his daughter," Roxy said.

"We understand," said Quincy.

Kimama ran to her father and took him in her arms. He grimaced and gently climbed down from his horse. "Thank you, my friends. Thank you."

"What happened in there?" asked Roxy.

Quincy and Porter looked to each other with world weary eyes. Quincy answered, "We don't want to talk about it, suffice to say, it's over."

Pointing at the bound and sacked Mala Cosa, Roxy asked, "Is that who I think it is? He stinks."

Porter agreed, "Yes, he does."

"And what happened to you? You look like you became a butcher for the evening."

"Maybe I did."

"We have to get you cleaned up."

"I hear you. I'll take care of it as best I can."

Chief Dan rode up and said, "You have done us many favors, taking care of great evils that nested in our lands."

"Seems like you all could have taken care of this yourselves," said Quincy.

"Yes, but why not get a white man to do the dirty work," he laughed.

"Too right," laughed Quincy.

28. Affliction

Porter held his breath while he bound the old sorcerer up like he was rolling up a map. Once Porter was sure the bindings were secure, he picked the dirty man up and stuck him on top of a mule. The animal was none too happy to have the smelly man upon his back, but being old and tired, it didn't put up too much of a fight either.

Roxy insisted they take the sack off his head, but agreed to let them keep his mouth suppressed with the bandana.

"We make our way due northwest and skirt alongside these mountains. Then we'll get back on the Old Spanish Trail and that will take us overland back to the Elk Mountain Mission—I mean Negro Bill's fort and from there back to Ferry-Town, Price and Salt Lake City. I'm anxious to see what Brother Brigham has to say about this wicked old scut."

Quincy agreed, "I've never seen old Brother Brigham but I've heard tales. I'd like to see what he says to this thing."

"Well, let's get a move on, we still have a long way to go."

They traversed the deserts rolling grasslands with ease this time, only occasionally having to move through a few rocky hills, until they were beside the mountains and had some shelter from the sun. They passed by various streams every now and again, making water not as much of an issue as it had been earlier that week on the lower sections of the Spanish Trail. For that fact, they were truly blessed.

It was strange, but as they moved along in a train of horses, Porter began feeling sore. A lot more bodily sore than usual. Sure, he was getting older he figured, but why was this hitting him now? Especially when the trail was relatively easy, he was on a good horse and he wasn't dehydrated.

They made good progress, but by mid-afternoon Porter found himself sitting gingerly in the saddle and falling farther behind the others. He had to ease over rocky outcroppings and make his horse slow down for each possible stirring jog on the path.

The others noticed his hesitancy and slow nature. He assured them he was all right and urged them to keep going and not wait up for him. By evening, he had fallen nearly a mile behind and when he caught up to them at the bottom of a red butte, they were already making camp.

Roxy brought him supper and gave him a warm drink. She put a cool hand to his forehead. "You feel all right, I don't think you have a fever," she said.

"I'm fine, just saddle sore I suppose. Maybe the last couple days have caught up to me is all."

She gave him a disbelieving look, but went back to see to the others. Redbone was still in a terrible way himself, but even the terribly wounded Ute chieftain had been able to keep up on the trail. That grated at Porter, but he couldn't push himself any harder than he was. He hadn't ever felt this uncomfortable in the saddle.

He glanced across the camp and saw Senor Mala Cosa staring balefires at him.

Porter frowned and gave him a dirty look and the old sorcerer finally turned away. But what really got Port's goat was the old man seemed to be smiling beneath his bandana, as if he was pleased at Port's discomfort.

The next morning, they roused themselves and prepared for the rest of the journey. Porter thought for a moment that someone had bound him up in rawhide, his body was so sore and stiff. "What the deuce?"

It was all he could do, to just rouse himself from his bedroll. His eyes ached and his hands felt like the blood had been drawn from them. He got to his knees and flexed his hands, making fists with them and stretching them in and out and back again.

"You all right?" asked Roxy.

"I'm right as rain," he said, barely able to stand erect. "Just make sure everyone else is getting ready, we're burning daylight."

"Are you sure? Did you get some kind of wound that you aren't telling me about?"

"I don't have a scratch on me."

Roxy grunted, but went off to see to the others.

"You look awful pale, Mr. Rockwell," said Emily.

"Tain't nothing I haven't been through before," he said, with a smile. "I'm just feeling a little chill." That was a lie, but he wasn't one to complain or show any amount of weakness. Especially since old Mala Cosa was still staring at him like a jaybird. Porter was tempted to shoot that smirk of his face then and there, but, realizing the company he was with, he refrained.

They were on the trail and passing through a brilliant red land. Here and there high mesas dropped up and down and even a great arch loomed beside the trail, catching the moon within its center like a great eye.

Porter again found himself riding so gingerly in the saddle that he was far behind the rest of them. His bones ached, his hands shook and a dizzying wave of nausea rode roughshod in his stomach. He imagined miners with dying canaries, crying aloud that something was about to give. Pain throbbed at his guts and more than once he nearly lost his grip on the reins. If they had been attacked by hostiles of any kind, he wasn't sure he would be capable of even drawing his gun.

This was a strange, maddening fear a helplessness he was altogether unfamiliar with. It was an alien realm he now rode through and the gnawing fear was that Mala Cosa was somehow behind it. But how?

It was dusk and Quincy rode up. "I was worried. Thought I'd have to pick you up and bring you back."

All Porter could do was grunt at him. Quincy wheeled his horse about and hollered something to the others.

From what senses Porter could discern, they had found a good place with a few trees beside a swift moving brook. High red cliffs behind them gave a sense of shelter and the wind was peaceful and just the right kind of cool. But Porter didn't feel cool, he hardly felt anything. It was sheer will and determination which kept him in the saddle at all. He nodded to Quincy who was still nearby.

"You don't look too good. I'm going to go get you some tonic," said Quincy.

Porter was sure now that he was knocking at death's door. A proud man, he didn't want to be pitied at his last moments, he didn't want to be thought of as weak. No, he would lie down and pass in his sleep. This seemed like a nice place. He wouldn't mind it being his last resting place. Too bad he couldn't tell the family back home goodbye, but life was what it was. The thought came to him that the blessing he had received from Joseph so long ago was still true. He had never been shot, never been stabbed. Of course, it would be some kind of sorcery that would finally lay him low like this. What else could it be?

He dropped from his horse and wasn't sure how he had even remained standing. It bought him time as Roxy, Emily and Kimama, glanced at him but no one approached yet. One of them called that they would bring him supper soon, but Porter couldn't even tell who had said it. His eyes were partially swollen shut and he couldn't see any better than he could hear.

He dropped down beside a tree and pondered closing his eyes forever. Then he looked and saw that Mala Cosa asleep, not more than twenty paces away. He was still bound hand and foot, but the bandana had slipped from his mouth. Considering he was asleep no one else had noticed yet. The black-hearted, old man was snoring beside a tree, not far from the babbling brook. Sure now the old sorcerer was the source of his woes, Porter crawled toward the old man, thinking he would wring the life from him with his last vestiges of strength.

Inch by inch, Porter crawled, using his elbows and knees. He could barely open his hands, they were of almost no use at all. His fingers were swollen and he had trouble even making a fist. Still he thought he would become the wild savage one last time to eradicate this paragon of evil.

Mala Cosa was laying on his back, asleep. His coarse, stringy hair splayed out about him like the branches of a dead tree. The deep wrinkles about his face held dirt and grime. While Porter's other senses were failing him, unfortunately, scent was not one of those. The old wizards reek was something to behold. He smelled of death and carnage, mayhem and brimstone, offal and rot. A more despicable person, Porter could not imagine.

Still, as Porter crawled forth at him, the old man turned in his sleep, revealing a piece of leather string dangling from a hidden pocket beneath his poncho.

Thinking that it might be Mala Cosa's medicine pouch, Porter grabbed it. Near as he could tell, it felt like it had small hard things inside maybe pebbles or even teeth, and most disturbing of all, a few long black hairs peeked from the top where it was cinched shut. Porter was positive they were his very own hairs that the sorcerer had collected to work some kind of devilish black magic upon him. He flung it as far away from himself as he could manage. It landed in the babbling brook.

With the splash, Porter began to feel better. He saw the bag floating away on the stream, disappearing in the clear waters.

Mala Cosa sprang awake, though bound hand and foot he lunged upward as best he could.

"Porter! You stole my conjure bag!"

"Did I now? Is that what that was?"

"I must have it back!"

"Like Hell, you wicked old cuss."

"I can't work my magic's anymore! You must get it back for me, and I will remove my curse upon you!"

Porter was already feeling better, the dark circles in his vision were departing and his hearing was restored.

"Please. Unchain me for I will follow you like a dog. I will be as your servant, just return to me my conjure bag," pleaded Mala Cosa.

The others had gathered about now and were astonished at the old sorcerer's sudden change in demeanor.

"Did I just hear what I thought I heard?" asked Roxy.

Porter struggled to stand, but made it on his own as the others reached him and put their hands on his elbows and back.

"I'm all right, getting better every moment, now that his black magic is getting washed away."

"What happened?" they asked at once.

Porter braced himself against the tree and said, "Somehow, old Mala Cosa here got a hold of some of my hair. He put it in his medicine pouch to bewitch me. That's why I felt so terrible. His magic was working on me something fierce."

"But is it over now?" asked Quincy. He glanced at the filthy old sorcerer and made as if he would strike him down.

"How could he do that? You're a Christian, that pagan magic shouldn't hold any sway on you!" sputtered Roxy.

Porter laughed. "We'd all like to think that, but there are some awful strange things in this world. I need a drink."

"I'll get you some water," offered Emily.

"Coffee?" offered Quincy.

"Nope. Get me some of my whiskey."

Roxy frowned.

"Please," said Porter, looking sheepishly from one woman to the other.

"Without my conjure bag," lamented Mala Cosa, "I can work no more magic. I am as other men. Please, slay me and end my travels on this earth. Let me go into the next world."

"Hell no. You're going before the judge of the land and we are going to find out all we can about your crimes. You are gonna be served some justice."

Mala Cosa slumped back down with his head in his hands. The stringy grey hair covered his features, but it sounded as if he were weeping.

No one had pity for him and the smell was still atrocious so they all slowly backed away and returned to the campfire upwind.

"Is this nightmare really over?" asked Emily. "Are the dark things he worked to bring about all done?"

"So far as I can tell. All I know is once that bag touched the water, I started to feel a whole lot better. And with as upset as he is, I sure hope it's the complete truth and that he has been castrated of all magical abilities."

Quincy laughed. "You got a way with words, Yankee."

"The power of language has its limits. It took throwing that damn bag to the four winds to break this."

"Not the winds," Roxy corrected, "but the purity of water."

"Whichever. It's done."

29. Reunion

As they approached the final stretch before they entered the valley and passed by the Elk Mountain Mission, Porter's curiosity got the better of him. He rode alongside the trundled Mala Cosa and asked, "Tell me about that spell you put on me."

Mala Cosa had lost all sense of grim superiority and vengefulness. "It was not a spell. It was a bewitching. You would have been dead before we reached the fort, of that I am sure."

"You disappointed?"

Mala Cosa sulked in the saddle. "It is done. I can work no more."

Quincy rode up beside Porter asking, "I imagine Bill is going to be awful upset. What are your plans on keeping the peace?"

Porter shrugged. "We offer him what we can, I suppose. The man is entitled to be paid fairly for a boat."

"You suggesting we pool some of our gold together?"

"That'd be fair."

Quincy frowned. He didn't like Bill and was hoping to hang onto as much coin as possible. "Couldn't you say we had to requisition it for deputy service?"

"I could, but not paying him wouldn't be honest. Sides we want him to have a flat boat. What if we ever need to come down here and requisition it again?"

Quincy furrowed his brow and shook his head, saying, "You cold, Yankee."

"Stop calling me that, Quint."

"And you stop calling me, Quint!"

"Maybe I will."

Mala Cosa groaned. "Kill me now."

They rode along the high red-rock cliffs as the valley opened before them, making good time and reaching the fort by noon.

Frenchie was out front, working on a butter churn. "Les enfants prodigue sont revenus."

Emily rode ahead asking, "Where's momma?"

Frenchie was about to answer when Bill stepped outside the doors. "Well, well, well. If it isn't the boat thieves."

Porter called out, "Bill, we'll give you some restitution. I didn't know they cheated you."

Bill snorted. "Don't look at me and tell me that rain ain't wet and the sky isn't up! You knew damn well they were getting me drunk so you could take the flatboat. You probably put them up to it!"

"Believe what you like but I that's not how it was. I didn't want them sharing my whiskey with anyone. Let alone you."

Bill's still glared at them, but then a smile crossed his face as he said, "I expect you'll keep your word and pay me something good for it?"

"I will. We have funds with us right now, as a matter of fact."

"Well come on in and take a load off then."

They sat around the central fire in the courtyard and ate a wild turkey for dinner. They kept Mala Cosa tied up outside the fort, but did bring him some scraps to eat, though he refused it.

Talk went over their river adventure and through the desert, and, of course, the strange man they had tied up outside and the ultimate fate of Matamoros.

Bill listened, but didn't mention anything of what had happened while they were away until Emily could take no more.

"Where is my Momma and sisters?"

Bill's mood visibly darkened. "Well, some deputy name of Brody Shaw came here just as you all left. He stayed on til the morning and took the ladies with him. He had quite an ax to grind against you Port. He seemed to think he was going to find some evidence against you relating to something that went down with the ladies. You know wherever you rescued them from."

"You mean killing nine of those slavers?"

"That's about the size of it," agreed Bill.

"But Mr. Rockwell saved us from them. We were bound to become sacrifices for the old wizard out there. He was gonna do blood magic on us!" shouted Emily.

"You don't gotta convince me. I'm just the messenger," said Bill.

Frenchie grunted his agreement. "Oui."

Porter rubbed at his beard. "Well, it will get sorted out. With the ladies as witnesses I don't imagine any jury in the territory would convict me."

"You're forgetting something. Shaw was taking it into consideration that you kidnapped the girl here."

"Me? I was a stowaway on the flatboat."

"I ain't the judge though," said Bill.

"I hear ya," said Porter. "Shaw is going to get Judge Spicer to put a warrant out for my arrest for kidnapping the girl plus any so-called evidence he can find on the Matamoros gang."

"You mean there are bodies that Redbone didn't hide?" asked Roxy.

Bill's eyebrows raised high at that remark. "Your wounded Indian friend there hides bodies for you?"

"It ain't like that. But yeah, he never did a thing with what was left of that wagon, and I was in such a hurry to get back to you all that I freed the women and told them to ride here since I couldn't take care of them."

Bill laughed. "This rabbit hole just gets deeper and deeper don't it, Frenchie?"

"Oui."

"You goading me, Bill? Cause I'm telling you that I am innocent of whatever Shaw told you, regardless of how this sounds."

Bill grinned. "You don't gotta tell me. I heard it from all those ladies time and again for a week, how you came riding in and shot those polecats all to hell, all by yourself. You are innocent of any wrongdoing there. Hero even. But the name Porter Rockwell and innocent, those two don't go hand in hand with anybody but you Mormons. No, Shaw and Spicer, I'm sure they want to see you hang and they'll find any reason to do it."

Porter frowned.

Bill clapped him on the shoulder. "Don't worry about right now though. Get some sleep tonight and worry about it in the morning."

30. Pain and Loss

They left that next morning with their pockets lightened by a good sum to pay Bill for the flatboat. It was a lot more than they would have liked, but Porter insisted they didn't want to make an enemy of Bill Granstaff.

They took a shortcut and ended up in Crescent Junction by nightfall and had a fire that they sat around, but spoke little. In the morning, Redbone and Kimama bid them farewell and rode off to meet up with their clan. That left the five of them including Mala Cosa who still refused to eat. He was barely conscious as they rode along toward Ferry-Town and twice he nearly slumped and fell off the mule.

"He looks like he is gonna die," said Quincy.

"Well, I can't make him eat," grumbled Porter.

"We need him to stay alive when we bring him before a judge," said Roxy.

"I know, but I can't make him eat."

"Well, maybe we could ask him nicely," suggested Emily.

"You do it, I'm done with him," said Porter.

They stopped beside the Green River, waiting for the ferry. Emily spoke softly to Mala Cosa, urging him to drink from a canteen.

He was unresponsive.

"He can't even hold it. Maybe if I—"

"No. He stays bound. Tip the water for him if you want, but he is not to be released or loosened or anything. Got it?" Porter said sternly.

Emily murmured that she had heard.

The ferry reached them and they boarded. Everyone was dismounted except for Mala Cosa who didn't appear to be awake.

"Where do you suppose, we'll see Shaw next?" asked Roxy.

"Hard to say. He is gonna be somewhere he'll think he can get the drop on me. Could be right here in Ferry-Town or maybe Price, maybe right as I ride back into Spanish Fork Canyon on my way north and home to the Point of the Mountain."

Mala Cosa was mumbling and Emily again held the canteen up for him.

His dry lips hardly took any water and he leaned forward in the saddle getting into a better position for more.

Emily stole a glance at the others as they stood, speaking against the rail. She leaned in to hold the canteen as high as she could for him.

Like a striking serpent, Mala Cosa sprung at the girl and was off the saddle. He had his bound hands over her neck and pressed against her throat, strangling her.

Her face turned blue and the fight was already out of her.

Porter realized what was happening, drew his six-gun and struggled to get around the horses to reach them. Roxy and Quincy did the same.

Mala Cosa swung the girl in front of himself, using her as shield. He knew Porter was a good enough marksman he would take a head shot. But he wouldn't if he feared he might hit the girl.

"Let her go!"

Mala Cosa grinned, his devilish broken teeth and his black eyes shined like obsidian. "I will not go to the white man's jail. I take her with me." He stepped back to jump into the river.

172

Porter shot him in the head, just as he leapt backward, his hands and bindings still wrapped about Emily's throat. They plunged into the dark brown waters and vanished.

Roxy screamed. Porter tossed his gun to Quincy and dove into the torrent.

He was swept away downstream but continually dove down again and again, searching for Emily. Nearing the bend in the river, he too disappeared from view.

Before the ferry even reached the shoreline, Roxy and Quincy were racing downstream after Porter. Almost a mile downstream, he dragged himself out of the river, without Emily.

"I couldn't—I couldn't find her." He sagged onto the bank in a heap, coughing up river water.

"Stay with him," said Quincy. He raced farther downstream until he too disappeared around a rocky bend.

"I can't believe I let that happen," Porter said. "I thought that old bastard was almost dead."

"It's not your fault. You tried." Roxy wiped away the tears herself. She looked downstream hoping for Quincy to return with the girl but hope seemed impossible.

Quincy came riding back alone. All he could do was shake his head.

They sat beside the river a long time. When dusk came, they finally rode into Ferry-Town and Porter went straight for the saloon.

Epilogue:

Porter called for a drink, the barkeep put down a tumbler, but Port took the bottle and guzzled it down in an instant.

"Porter! You can't! That won't help anything. It won't bring her back!" Roxy argued. She tried in vain to take the bottle from him.

"Then it won't matter if I have another!" he roared.

Roxy made to argue, but Quincy held her back. "Let him deal with it his own way. As a matter of fact, I need to join him. I was beginning to like that little blonde."

A second bottle later, Porter was at least sitting at the table. The oil lamps cast long, dark shadows on his face, giving a sinister dark edge to his countenance. He called for a third bottle, slurring the words.

Roxy and Quincy sat at the table next to him, each lost in their own somber thoughts.

"Well, look at this," said a familiar voice. Shaw stood in the doorway, grinning. "Who would have thought it could be this easy?"

Quincy and Roxy made to draw their guns, but Shaw's posse was all around them. Six guns pointed at them. "Take them all into custody," he said.

Porter stared up with crazed eyes.

"I've got you now, Porter Rockwell. I've got all the evidence I need. Bodies of those innocent men you killed in the desert. Witnesses for a mutilated little Indian girl and where is the girl you kidnapped? Did she meet the same fate?"

Mae Taggart stormed into the saloon. "Where is my daughter? She'll tell you that Mr. Rockwell did not kidnap her!" She saw Rockwell sitting at the table, with three bottles beside him. "Where is Emily? Is she all right?"

Porter just looked at her with sad silent eyes.

"Where is she?" She sobbed, then screamed. "Where is she? Where is my daughter?"

"Stay back, Ms. Taggart. He is a thoroughly dangerous man. You gonna draw on me, Porter?"

Porter began to stand. He tipped a little to one side as if he were aboard a sailing ship. His hand slowly reached for his gun, then the crazed look in his eye vanished and he fell forward on his face, hitting the floor.

"Seems like that's all the confession I need," said Shaw. He put handcuffs on the unconscious Porter. "He is gonna hang this time!"

The End
but
Porter rides again in
You Only Hang Once
Coming Soon

David J. West

Acknowledgments

Thanks to my wife Melissa Adrina West, and Jana S. Brown, Jay Barnson, Erin West, John Olsen, Nathan Shumate, Anna Stansfield, Bryce Beatty, Kevin Molett, Dave Butler and the Space Balrogs, and plenty of others that need to forgive me for not naming them here. Thank you all for your help.

About the Author:

   David J. West writes dark fantasy and weird westerns because the voices in his head won't quiet until someone else can hear them. He is a great fan of sword & sorcery, ghosts and lost ruins, so of course he lives in Utah in with his wife and children.

   You can visit him online at:

http://www.kingdavidjwest.com/

https://twitter.com/David_JWest

http://david-j-west.tumblr.com/

Also by David J. West

Dark Trails Saga
Six-Gun Serenade
Cold Slither
Whispers Out of the Dust
Fangs of the Dragon
SCAVENGERS

And Coming Soon

You Only Hang Once

Lit Pulp Collection
Weird Tales of Horror
The Mad Song: and other Tales of Sword & Sorcery
Gods in Darkness
Whispers of the Goddess
The Hand of Fate

Eldritch Collection
Space Eldritch
Space Eldritch 2: The Haunted Stars
Redneck Eldritch

Heroes of the Fallen Saga
Heroes of the Fallen
Bless the Child
Blood of Our Fathers (forthcoming)

Reviews are always appreciated, thanks for reading and to hear about news, special giveaways and deals - Sign up for Burnt Offerings and get a free ebook!